# ALEXA
## Crushed

ALEXA SERIES BOOK ONE

## T.R. CUPAK

xoxo

D1445932

This book is a work of fiction. Names, characters, places, and incidents either are the product of the author's imagination or are used fictitiously, and any resemblance to actual persons, living or dead, events, or locales is entirely coincidental.

Written for ages eighteen and older due to adult language and graphic sexual content.

ISBN-13: 978-1511735391
ISBN-10: 1511735392

Cover Design by Tugboat Design
Interior Formatting by Tugboat Design

# Prologue

It was October 15 and also my second birthday when my mother walked out on my dad and me. Sylvia Morgan was a selfish person who had many dark issues surface after I was born. Once she had to compete for my father's attention, she began to go crazy. She was insanely jealous of me, her own daughter, and kept threatening my dad that she was going to leave us.

My father, Joseph Morgan, was thirty-four years old and the lead mechanical engineer for a classified weapons manufacturing company in Silicon Valley. Not only was my dad extremely intelligent, but he was also very loving and handsome. Joseph stood six feet two with an olive skin tone and an intimidating muscular build. He looked like the man you would avoid passing on a dark street, but looks could be deceiving. The badass persona contradicted the true man. His jet-black hair was cut short, but you could still see a hint of the natural wave in it. His chocolate-brown eyes were soft and warm in contrast to the starkness of his jet-black hair.

When my mother slammed the front door for the very last time, Joseph was actually glad she had finally left. My dad loved me very much and worried for my safety when Sylvia was around. Her jealousy knew no boundaries. Her leaving was perfect timing since he was already preparing to divorce her. Of course, being only two years old at the time, I don't remember her leaving. I found out about her later in my life.

On January 3, there was a knock at the door sometime in the early evening. My dad had been home from work for a little bit and was changing to work out down in the basement when he went to answer the front door, finding two police officers standing there. The first officer to speak was Officer Helton.

"Good evening, sir. Are you Joseph Morgan?" the officer asked.

My dad looked at the man with utter confusion and said, "Yes, Officer. Is something the matter?"

"May we come in and speak with you, Mr. Morgan?" the second officer, introduced as Sergeant Norton, replied.

"Yes, please come in and have a seat. Can I get either of you coffee or water?"

"No, thanks. We're fine," Sergeant Norton replied. He didn't waste any time and immediately asked, "Sir, is your wife Sylvia Morgan?"

"Yes, she is. I'm not sure what this is about, but she left my daughter, Alexa, and me back on October 15. We haven't heard from her or seen her since then. Is she in trouble?"

Sergeant Norton continued, "Earlier today, we found your wife dead in a hotel room not too far from here. It looks as if she possibly overdosed a couple of days ago. There were a couple of used syringes, a tourniquet around her arm, a spoon, a lighter, and a few packets of heroin lying next to her on the bed. There were also prescription medications and half a bottle of whiskey on the nightstand as well. There were no signs of foul play, and it looked as if she was the only one staying in the room."

Joseph sat in silence with a look of shock and disbelief on his face. Both officers gave my dad a chance to process the information he had just been given.

"Mr. Morgan, we will need you to come down to the morgue to

identify your wife's body," Officer Helton said. "Do you want to do that now or in the morning?"

My dad still sat silent for a few moments and then looked to both officers sitting across from him and said, "I'll do it now. Let me go next door and see if my neighbor can watch Alexa for me. I, of course, do not want to take her to the morgue."

"We understand, sir. That's not a problem. We can wait for you."

Just then, I walked into the living room, rubbing my eyes sleepily. "Daddy, I hungy."

"OK, princess. Daddy has to go with these two nice officers somewhere, but I will see if Mrs. Logan can watch you for a little bit. I'm sure she will have your favorite—macaroni and cheese."

"Yay!" I squealed.

# Chapter One

My dad met Jeanine Langley nine months after my mother, Sylvia, was found dead in a hotel room from a drug overdose. They met at a swanky new restaurant in downtown Palo Alto. My dad had a business dinner meeting with the head of his department, and as he was walking by the very busy bar area on his way out, he spotted a stunningly beautiful woman sitting at the end of the bar, lost in her thoughts.

Jeanine Langley was thirty years old and already a well-established architect. She owned her own business, which did extremely well in booming Silicon Valley. She was a beautiful woman with her five-foot-seven slender frame; porcelain skin; long, wavy blond hair; and eyes that were green like emeralds. She kept herself in extremely good shape with Pilates and swimming. Earlier in the day, Jeanine found out she could never have children, which was why she was sitting at the end of the bar, drinking alone, lost in thought.

Everything happened so fast after my dad approached Jeanine. They were married at the courthouse in Fremont within a month. Not only did Jeanine fall madly in love with my dad, but she instantly fell in love with me too. Being that she couldn't have children of her own, she was thrilled when my dad told her he was a single father to the most precious two-going-to-be-three-year-old princess who had golden-brown hair, soft honey-brown eyes, and olive-toned skin that matched his own. My dad was thankful that with each day I looked more like him than my biological mother.

We moved in with Jeanine in her quaint but updated Craftsman-style house in Fremont the day of the wedding. Our new house sat on a wide street that was lined with beautiful mature oak trees. The house wasn't a cookie-cutter home like most in developments are now. Each house was unique and charming, adding to the appeal of our new neighborhood. It truly was the perfect neighborhood to grow up in.

Two weeks after the wedding, finally having my dad and me settled, Jeanine threw a party for close friends and neighbors. She wanted everyone to meet the new loves of her life. George and Marie Miller lived across the street, and they had a son, Devin, who was my age. This was the first time I met my soon-to-be best friend. Sadly, I was the only little girl on the block. Everyone had sons. The Johnsons had three boys—Matthew was three, Marc was four and a half, and Mitchell was six. There was also the Wyles' son, Robbie, who was four.

I was never a shy kid. How could I be with a father who was always dragging me everywhere with him? I asked the other kids if they wanted to play in my room. They all followed me down the hall to my new room. I walked in first, and Devin was right behind me. The other boys stopped at the door, as if they were afraid to walk into a room that boasted a pink-and-white canopy bed, a white dresser and nightstand, and a play kitchen in the corner with a small dining table that had my tea party set sitting on it from my last stuffed animal and dolly tea party. My walls were a pale pink with dark purple Chevron stripes and a mural that simply read "PRINCESS" as an accent piece.

Mitchell, being the oldest, said, "I'm not going in there! Everything is pink and probably has cooties. I'm going to play in the backyard."

His brothers of course agreed in unison, and they all headed out to the backyard with Robbie Wyle in tow. Devin stayed behind. He didn't say anything, but he looked around, touching my things here and there, and then spotted my bin of LEGOs. He walked over to it, pulled it out, and dumped the LEGOs out onto my floor. We sat in silence and began building something. At three years old, you really don't know what you're building; you just want it bigger and taller than you. That was the beginning of our friendship.

## Nine Years Later

As my twelfth birthday approached, I thought back to how growing up on a street with all boys changed me. I quickly learned that I had to ditch the frilly dresses, dolls, and Barbies and ask for a PlayStation, skateboard, and BMX bike. Even though I gradually became a tomboy and was now being called Alex by the Johnson brothers, I was still a princess at heart. I didn't care though, since they had finally accepted me. Devin, who was three months older and about three inches taller, had sandy-blond hair, baby-blue eyes, and tan skin because we were always outside. He called me Lexi, like my mom did. Robbie Wyle, a short, scrawny redhead with lots of freckles, could never think for himself, so, depending on who was around, my name was always different for him.

But Devin was my best friend, and we were always together because our parents were always together as well. If our families weren't camping, vacationing, or partying together at one another's houses, then Devin and I would either be throwing a football around, playing catch with a baseball, or riding our bikes around the neighborhood pretending we were the Goonies. When that would get boring, we would just hang out watching scary movies, even when we weren't supposed to. Our moms thought we were still too young, but our dads thought differently. Come to think of it, our dads loved scaring the crap out of us every chance they got. It's no wonder they didn't mind letting us watch all those scary movies.

Recently, my dad was given a huge promotion at work with a hefty pay increase, and my mom's architect firm had doubled in size and business over the last couple of years. It was four days before my twelfth birthday, and we were almost finished packing up our house to move across the bay to Hillsborough. Even though it was only thirty-one miles from Fremont to Hillsborough, it might as well have been three thousand miles when you couldn't drive yet and there was a body of water that separated you from your best friend. Our parents kept telling us that things wouldn't change and that everything would be the same, but how could they tell us that when Devin and I were going from seeing each other every day to barely at all?

"Alexa, stop moping. You have your laptop, iPad, and cell phone. You and Devin can Skype, text, Facebook, and whatever else your generation does to stay in contact," my dad said. "Besides, I've seen you guys sitting outside together, but you're both communicating via your phones. How would this be different?"

"It's different because we can't hang out every day, Dad!" At this point, I was struggling to keep my composure. I never cried, and I wasn't going to start now. The move really was going to suck.

"Princess, it's going to be fine. You haven't even seen the new house yet. I promise you will love it, and once we are settled, we will have the Millers over."

I had turned my back on my dad even though I was listening to everything he was saying, but I was still pouting and not proud of that fact. I put my headphones on, turned on my iPod, and finished packing the last of my room while Britney sang to me.

I was lost in thought, thinking that the other sucky thing about this move was the timing. I wouldn't get to spend my birthday with

Devin. We had plans to go go-kart racing and hit the batting cages in Newark, and after that, we were going to come back to my house, make a bunch of Jiffy Pop popcorn, and veg out watching the entire Nightmare on Elm Street movie series. Those were our favorite, since we lived on Elm Street.

I felt a tap on my shoulder that made me jump and found my mom standing behind me with a cautious look on her face. I took off my headphones and just hugged her. I didn't need to say anything. She already knew I was sad.

She kissed the top of my head, brought her hands down to cup my face, and looked lovingly at me with her emerald eyes. She said, "Lexi, you will see Devin. This isn't the end of the world." She removed her hands from my face and placed them on top of my shoulders and continued, "How about I take you clothes shopping at Stanford Mall for your birthday? You are starting a new school just after the semester has started, and I would love for you to dress more like the beautiful young girl you are and not hide your beauty under a 49ers cap, jeans, T-shirts, and Vans that you wear now so you can fit in with the boys on this street."

Mom always knew what to say and how to say it. I saw the hope in her eyes after she asked me to go shopping. All I could do was look up at her, smile, and nod.

"Great!" she said, smiled, and gave me another quick hug before leaving my room.

It was amazing that when you want time to slow down, it flies by even faster. Today was moving day, and Devin and I were sitting on the bottom stair of my porch.

"Well, this really sucks," Devin said. "Now I'm stuck dealing with the idiot Johnson brothers and their minion, Robbie, all by myself."

I couldn't help but chuckle at Devin's last remark. "It's not like I'm the one choosing to move, Dev." Sounding defeated, I continued, "I just don't know why we have to move at all. Dad still works at the same place, and so does Mom. They keep telling me that it's time for change and that the schools are, like, way better in Hillsborough, and I will be getting a top-notch junior high and high school education in a public school, blah, blah, blah. Big whoop!"

"So does that mean I'm going to be stupider than you because I'm getting an education in Fremont's public schools?"

"You're already stupider than me, Dev. We both know that." We laughed for a quick second as we playfully bumped shoulders, and then reality was back. "Who cares? School is school. It doesn't matter where you go."

We heard a throat-clearing sound from behind us, and we both turned and looked up to see my dad standing on the porch with his arms crossed. "It sure does matter where you go to school, young lady. Especially when it is time to submit to colleges," he said matter-of-factly.

"Dad, I'm going to be twelve tomorrow. College is still a ways off."

"Alexa, I'm done having these conversations with you. Say your good-byes and get in the car. We need to get to the house before the movers arrive."

I looked back at Devin, and we both stood up at the same time. "Well, I guess this is it," I said. "Don't go turning into an idiot like the Johnson brothers or a minion like Robbie."

He smiled and said, "Don't you go turning into a snob from your ivory tower."

We gave each other a quick fist bump, and he left to go home as I went to the car. As soon as we pulled out of our driveway, I sent him a text.

Me: This sux!
Devin: YUP! Text when u reach the ivory tower.
Me: Whatev! What's w/ ivory tower comment?

Devin: Mvg up to high class that's what.
Me: UR an ASS
Devin: Right back @ ya

That was the last text for a while. I didn't know why Dev thought I was going to change just because I lived in a different city. I was still going to be the same ole Lexi.

As we turned down a street that had two large houses on each side, spread pretty far apart by their vast, gated front yards, I started to think that maybe I was wrong about changing. All that was going through my mind was, We're not in Kansas anymore. This street led to the end, which was a cul-de-sac with three more large houses equally as far apart as the others.

My dad pointed to the house on the far left and said, "That's our new home, princess."

My jaw dropped at the sight before me. The house was humongous. It definitely dwarfed our old Craftsman-style home back in Fremont. This house had a four-car garage with a separate driveway down the left side of the house leading toward the backyard. I wondered where that led to. Above the garage, it looked to have a balcony, and through the wrought-iron railing, I saw double doors leading out to it. I actually had a tinge of excitement building in me for the first time since I found out about our move.

Mom and Dad were both out of the car and approaching the stairs that led up to the custom, antique wood door. It looked like a door that would belong on a castle. My thoughts went immediately to Devin's ivory tower comment. I just sucked in a breath and shook my head.

As I started to walk toward the stairs, I heard the muffler of what sounded like a motorcycle. I stopped and glanced back at the street opening, and a red sport bike caught my attention. The rider flew down the street and pulled into the driveway of the house two over from us. Now that he was closer, I could see he was riding a Yamaha R1. I didn't know why I was staring, but I was. The rider took off his helmet and ran his free hand through his mussed dark hair. He looked to be in high school, maybe sixteen or seventeen years old. He looked over at me and caught me staring at him. My breath hitched, and I felt the blush running to my cheeks at the quizzical look he gave me. All I could tell from this distance was that he was hot and even hotter with his half-cocked smile. I was a pubescent twelve-year-old—well, would be tomorrow—and had grown up with a bunch of boys, but this one boy made my insides feel different. Where was this shyness and blushing coming from? I didn't do girlie stuff like this, like, ever.

"Lexi!" Mom yelled down from the stairs and pulled my attention away from the hottie next door. "Come on. We want to show you around the house before the movers arrive."

"I'm coming!" I yelled back, taking one last glance over at my new neighbor, who was still looking at me with the same curious look on his face. I started toward the door, and after a couple of steps, I tripped over my own feet. I stumbled but caught my balance before I fell. Oh my God, that did not just happen.

Mom was still standing at the top of the stairs, and she was looking at me with one of her perfect eyebrows cocked. She had noticed my bright-red face. She then glanced over at the boy with the cool motorcycle next door. A knowing smile flashed across her face. How my mom knew these things was beyond me, but she tried to ease my embarrassment by simply whispering, "I don't think he saw you trip, Lexi." I glanced up at her, all doe-eyed, but she just smiled.

We went inside, and I was immediately taken aback by how large this house was. Even though the house looked to be only two stories from the outside, when you walked in the front door, it was actually three levels. We were standing by the sunken living room that was off to the right of the foyer, with an attached, raised formal dining room off of it. The massive eat-in gourmet kitchen was directly in front of us, and it overlooked the family room below. To the left of us were a set of stairs leading up to the third level and another set leading down to the lower-level family room.

Dad was at the top of the stairs with a huge smile on his face. "Come on, princess. We want to show you your room."

I ascended the stairs. My dad was waiting next to the double doors on the left, and he opened them both and stepped inside, and I just poked my head around the wall into the room. My mouth dropped as I looked at the huge room. Directly across from my double doors to the bedroom entrance were the French doors leading out to the balcony I'd seen as we drove up. To the left of my bedroom doors was a decent-sized area that would definitely fit my full-size bed. Actually, it would dwarf it. To the right of my bedroom doors, I saw two separate doors that were side by side and still closed. I opened the one that was closest to me, and, to my surprise, it was my very own walk-in closet. "Wow," I whispered. I was glad I'd agreed to go clothes and shoe shopping with my mom so I could fill this closet, which was almost as big as my old bedroom back in Fremont.

Mom was standing by the second door, and she smiled. "If you like that, then you will love this," she said as she opened the second door and stepped back. I walked over, and I was staring at my very own bathroom. It had a double vessel sink with glass bowls in earthy colors mounted on granite countertops with a makeup vanity between them. The shower was massive. It had body jets and a rain showerhead. The Jacuzzi bathtub was separate, and it looked big enough that I could swim in it. I was completely speechless. I turned to look at both of my parents, who had huge smiles on their faces.

"This is really my room?" I asked. If they said no, I would be so mad that they got my hopes up.

"It sure is. You finally have a room that is meant for a princess,"

Dad said.

"My bedroom furniture is going to look silly in here, but I will make it work," I said in a whisper, looking down at my hands, fidgeting.

"Don't worry about that. Your father and I bought you a whole new bedroom set with a king-size bed and matching desk. Your room will be beautiful," Mom said with a sweet smile.

"Oh, my God!" I squealed, giving both of my parents a big hug. "This is awesome!" I yelled as I turned to walk out onto the balcony. I immediately looked down and saw hottie biker boy from next door putting on his helmet. As if he sensed me, he glanced up at the balcony and caught me staring, again. I immediately blushed, and he flipped his visor down so I couldn't see his eyes, but I knew he was still looking at me before he swung his leg over the bike, started the motor, backed it out of the driveway, and then sped off down the street and out of sight. Seriously, what was it with me? I shook my head.

Now that the hottie was gone and I was once again thoroughly embarrassed, I decided I wanted to see if the rest of the house was as awesome as my room. Directly across from my room were two separate doors. Both were bedrooms, but they were too small to be the master. At the end of the hall was a guest bathroom, which was nicely done with a double sink and shower/tub combo.

The moving truck and the furniture delivery truck had both arrived, and my parents were outside giving instructions while I continued to explore the house. I made my way down to the kitchen, which boasted dark wood cabinets, earthy-colored granite countertops like in my bathroom, and top-of-the-line stainless-steel appliances. The kitchen had a large picture window above the sink and another by the dining area. They faced the backyard, which seemed to go all the way back to the tree line. I headed down to the lower level. Right across from the stairs was another set of double doors leading to the master bedroom. I thought my room was amazing, but this one was fabulous. It had a sitting area with built-in cherrywood bookshelves, his and hers walk-in closets, and where my bathroom was spa-like my parents' looked to be made for royalty.

I walked to the end of the hall toward the front of the house, and to the left was a powder room. I opened the door immediately in front of me, and it opened to our four-car garage. Mom's Lexus was parked in the middle of the left side. Both sets of doors were open, and I saw the movers scurrying to get stuff off their trucks and into our house. I headed back inside toward the sliding glass door opposite the garage that leads out back. I walked out onto pavers and saw a huge swimming pool with lava rocks surrounding the back side of it and a waterfall off to the right that had the built-in hot tub attached. Behind the hot tub was the pool house with a bar setup. There was a large grassy area, and I immediately thought of Devin and wished he was there to explore with me. To the left of the pool, I saw another building that the second driveway I saw out front led to. I went over to see if the side door was unlocked, and it wasn't. Since the front of the additional building had a role-up door, I was sure it was probably another garage. Who needed so many garages?

I kicked off my shoes and sat at the edge of the pool with my feet in the water, and even though it was October, the water still felt warm. I chocked it up to the fact the pool must be heated. I grabbed my phone from my back pocket, took a quick picture, and sent it to Devin.

Me: Wish you could explore with me.
Devin: Damn! Is that your pool?
Me: Yup. Maybe next wkd u can come swim. It's heated!
Devin: Maybe. It's not like I can just walk over anymore.

Devin's text messages seemed distant, like he didn't want to talk to me.

Me: Movers are here. Have to start unpacking. TTYL
Devin: Later.

I shrugged off the feeling that even though it hadn't even been one day, my best friend didn't want to be my friend anymore.

❧

I woke up in my new room, in my new bed, in my new house, and it was my birthday. Even though I didn't have my best friend with me, the sun was shining through the French doors, and I wouldn't let it bother me too much. I swung my legs over the side of my bed, stretched, and headed over to my balcony. I walked outside and took in the fresh air as I leaned against the balcony railing. My eyes immediately glanced over to my hot neighbor's house and saw someone at the second-story window. I could feel the person staring at me. I shook my head and went back inside to brush my teeth so I could head to the kitchen.

When I came out of my room, I immediately smelled breakfast. Mom must have gotten up early to go to the store. There was no food in the house last night. We had ordered pizza for dinner. I half skipped down the stairs and into the kitchen. Dad was sitting at the dining table with a cup of coffee and reading the Sunday paper. Mom was cooking away at the stove.

"Well, there's the birthday girl," Dad said cheerfully over the rim of his newspaper.

Mom turned and held out her arm to give me a hug. "Happy birthday, Lexi," she said, kissing the side of my head.

"Thanks, guys. The food smells amazing. What's for breakfast? I'm starving!" I asked.

"Raisin bread French toast, bacon, extra crispy like you like it, and scrambled eggs with green onions," Mom said happily.

"Yum!"

"I also got you a sugar-free Red Bull. It's in the refrigerator." She nodded toward our massive new refrigerator.

"That's just what I need to wake me up."

My dad put his newspaper down and took a sip of his coffee. "I have a surprise for you after we eat breakfast."

As I sat at the table with my Red Bull, I looked at my dad with questioning eyes. "Surprise? I thought my bedroom furniture was my birthday gift."

He smiled. "It is, princess. This is something else."

"You guys spoil me. You know that, right?"

My parents laughed at my statement. Once we were all seated at the table eating breakfast, we carried on chatting between bites. After breakfast, I helped Mom clear the table, and Dad said, "Those can wait. Let's go see that other surprise."

He led us out back toward the other garage. He stopped us and told us to wait while he went inside to open the garage door.

"Surprise!" he exclaimed.

Mom and I looked in the garage, and we saw a car body, frame, boxes, a massive engine sitting on a crate, and four wheels leaned up against the back wall. We both tilted our heads and looked at my dad with questions in our eyes.

Dad saw we didn't understand and began to explain. "This is a Factory Five MK4 Roadster kit car. It's a replica of a '65 AC Shelby Cobra. It's a car I've always wanted but could never afford."

"Why is the car in pieces, Joseph?" Mom asked with her beautiful eyes staring lovingly at my dad.

Dad huffed and continued, "Even with the new job, we still can't afford a real one, and while I was searching online, I came across this website and thought why not build my dream car and have something we could do together as a family? I want us to build this car together, Jeanine."

Mom smiled sweetly at her husband. "I'm not one to get my hands dirty, but I will sit out here with the two of you, drink wine, and maybe hand you a tool." She chuckled.

"I'm in!" I exclaimed. "This will be freaking awesome when it's done, Dad!" I was actually excited about this. My dad's free time was minimal, and for him to suggest this meant I might have more of that father-daughter time.

"Well, let's get changed and get started," he said with a huge smile on his face.

It was later in the afternoon, and Dad and I were wrapping up organizing the boxes and parts of the kit car. Mom went inside within fifteen minutes of seeing Dad's new toy, using the excuse of wanting to continue to unpack. My phone chimed with a text.

Devin: Happy Birthday Lexi!
Me: Thanks Dev! Wish we could have kept our plans.
Devin: Me too. The idiot brothers keep teasing me.
Me: Screw them! They're just jealous you have an AWESOME bff and they're stuck w/ each other =)
Devin: Whatev
Me: Look at what my dad bought!

I snapped a quick picture and sent it.

Devin: Is that a car?
Me: Yes. It's a kit car of a '65 Shelby Cobra.
Devin: Cool. I gotta go. Have a great bday Lexi.
Me: Thanks =) Skype later?

Devin: Maybe

There was that word again—maybe. What was his deal?

Me: K. Later Dev

It had only been a day, but I really missed my best friend and his short texts were starting to irritate me.

"Was that Devin?" Dad asked.

"Yeah. He's being weird."

"Weird?" He looked at me quizzically.

"We always joke back and forth through text messages all day long, and since yesterday, he's been kinda distant."

"I wouldn't worry too much, princess. I'm sure he's just busy or just getting used to the change," my dad said, trying to cheer me up.

"Maybe. I'm going to go inside and get stuff ready for my first day of my new school tomorrow. Yay me," I said sarcastically.

"OK, Alexa."

It didn't take me long to get my school stuff together or to figure out what I was going to wear since I had stayed up late last night unpacking and organizing my room. I had to have everything in order and in its place, or I went crazy. I was pretty sure I took after my dad in this area. I mean, we just spent most of the day organizing the kit car and its parts in the order we had to build it in.

I went to sit out on my balcony and play Bejeweled Blitz on my iPad as the sun started to set. I heard the now familiar sound of the motorcycle getting close. I glanced up to see hottie biker boy speed down the street. I didn't know why, but I got a funny feeling in my stomach every time I heard his bike. I felt as if there were a million butterflies fluttering around in my stomach.

He pulled into his driveway and dismounted his bike. And just like yesterday, he took off his helmet, ran the fingers of his free hand through his dark hair, and, as if he felt me watching him, looked up at me with that same half-cocked smirk on his lips. I blushed instantly, as I was caught once again staring at hottie biker boy.

"Lexi, dinner," Mom called from downstairs.

I jumped up quickly, knocking my chair over, making a loud clang against the wrought-iron railing. "Dammit," I muttered under my breath.

Within seconds, Mom appeared across my room in the doorway. "Are you OK, Lexi? I heard a loud noise."

I glanced back down at biker boy, and he had a huge grin on his face. I narrowed my eyes, gave him a dirty look, and turned to look over my shoulder. "I'm fine. You scared me, and I jumped, knocking over my stupid chair."

She came closer to where I was standing and saw biker boy going into his house. She eyed me carefully and smiled. "You know, Lexi, he's a little too old for you. I'm guessing sixteen or seventeen."

"What are you talking about?" I asked, shocked.

"I was teenage girl once. I think I can spot a crush better than you can."

I felt my face heat up, and I couldn't even look my mom in the eye right then. Was that what this feeling was? A crush? Whatever it was, I wasn't OK with it. "Ugh, Mom. Don't say things like that."

"You're twelve now, and in another year, you'll be thirteen. Your body and hormones are changing. Boys will become a different interest as you get older. You won't want to ride a skateboard or play football with them anymore. You're going to want to kiss them."

"Enough, Mom! You're grossing me out right now," I said, exasperated.

She smiled. "Come on, Lexi. It's dinnertime. Your father is waiting for us."

We had just finished dinner and cleared the table when the doorbell rang. Dad was relaxing in the family room downstairs, watching some science show, and Mom dried her hands to go answer the door. I was on her heels, as I was heading back up to my room to see if I could get Devin to Skype.

"Hello. We're your neighbors from two houses over," said a female voice with a hint of elegance in it. "I'm Olivia Gage, and this is my husband, Victor, and son, Ethan."

I froze at the door to my room when I heard hottie biker boy's name. "This day is just getting better and better," I grumbled under my breath.

"Well, hello. I'm Jeanine Morgan. Please come in," my mom responded graciously.

"Thank you," a deep voice replied.

My dad came up the stairs from the family room, and I poked my head out of my bedroom door. I couldn't believe he was in my house right now.

"Olivia, Victor, and Ethan Gage, this is my husband, Joseph Morgan."

They all exchanged pleasantries, and my mom offered them drinks and a seat in our living room. My dad glanced to the top of the stairs and saw me peeking out of my bedroom.

"Alexa, come down and meet our neighbors, the Gages," he said.

I slowly descended the stairs, not wanting to trip and fall down them. That would have been just freaking fantastic if I had. Why not make a bigger ass of myself in front of hottie biker boy.

"This is our daughter, Alexa. Today is her twelfth birthday," Mom said with a pride in her voice that made me blush. What was with the blushing lately? It really needed to stop.

"Hello, Mr. and Mrs. Gage," I said as I went to shake their hands. I did have manners, as both of my parents had brought me to work and social events often enough that I did know how to act. Sometimes.

"Oh, please, Alexa, call me Olivia, and my husband is Victor. This is our sixteen-year-old son, Ethan."

"Hi, Ethan. I'm Lexi." I smiled and stuck my hand out for him to shake.

"Hey," he said with a lopsided smirk on his face as he grabbed my hand to shake. He had a strong grip, and the second he touched my hand, I felt the heat rise to my cheeks again. Stop blushing, I told myself.

I snatched my hand back, wanting to smack the smirk right off his face but thinking better of it as I crossed the living room to where my parents were seated. My mom was watching me closely and had that all-knowing smile on her face, since she seemed to think I had a crush on hottie—oh, wait, I had a name now—Ethan.

I was sitting across from Ethan, trying to take in his model good looks on the sly without being noticed. His close proximity allowed me to see more clearly that his hair was dark brown with a hint of auburn, cut shorter on the sides than the top, with slight waves through it. His full, dark eyelashes enhanced his steel-gray eyes, which flickered with amusement. He was wearing a tight black T-shirt that showed off the lean, muscular build beneath. His faded boot-cut jeans were tight in the right places, and he was still wearing his riding boots. I let out a sigh and didn't realize it was audible until all attention was focused on me.

"What was that, Alexa?" Dad asked.

"What? Huh? I didn't say anything," I said as my cheeks got hot again. I just wanted to die right there, right now.

Mom patted my knee as the conversation continued on after my embarrassing sigh. I was too scared to even look back at Ethan now, but I felt his eyes staring at my side profile. I should have just said, "Hi. Dorky preteen over here just wants to ogle over you." Crap, Mom was right. I was crushing. What the hell?

"Victor and I own Gage Real Estate Development. Our office is located in San Francisco," Olivia stated.

"Oh, I think my architecture firm did one of your tenant improvements in Palo Alto about six years ago," Mom chimed in. "Langley Architecture and Design, Inc."

"Yes, I believe you did," Olivia said politely. "Your firm did an amazing job redesigning the layout of that old building and completely changing the outdated outside facade to bring the building into this decade; it was absolutely breathtaking once it was completed."

"Thank you so much for thinking so. We aim to please our clients," Mom said with a smile.

"So you're Jeanine Langley?" Victor asked.

"Yes. Langley is my maiden name. I started the firm before I met and fell in love with this handsome man and his beautiful daughter," Mom answered, squeezing both of our hands in a show of affection.

"That's quite the accomplishment," he said to my mom. "So are you in the architect business too, Joseph?" Victor turned his attention to my dad.

"No. I'm actually the VP of a private weapons and defense company," Dad answered.

"Sounds top secret," Victor joked.

"It can be. I mean, it's no secret what we do at our facility. The top secret comes from the types of weapons design and manufacturing we do there," Dad said proudly.

"That's very impressive." Olivia's compliment sounding like a purr as she unabashedly took in my dad's handsome features. Was I the only one who caught that? I guess not since I just saw Ethan's body stiffen as he rolled his eyes at his mother's words.

"So do you and Victor have any other children besides Ethan here?" Mom asked Olivia.

I glanced over at Ethan and saw his body go rigid at my mom's question. Olivia's eyes quickly darted to Victor and then back to my mom. "Well, we've taken up plenty of your time. I'm sure you have more unpacking to do, and I should get my men back home. We just wanted to come over and welcome you to the neighborhood," she said, avoiding answering the question. Everyone stood at that point, and the Gages made their way to the front door.

"Thank you so much for coming over and introducing yourselves. We appreciate the hospitality," Mom said.

"We look forward to the housewarming party," Victor said as he shook my dad's hand.

"So do we," Dad said with a laugh.

"It was a pleasure meeting you, Alexa," Olivia said.

"Please, call me Lexi. And it was nice meeting you all as well," I said as politely as I could.

"Will do, Lexi."

Ethan was the last to walk by me, and he had a Cheshire grin as he reached out to grab my hand to shake it again. I was taken by surprise, and my cheeks immediately flushed crimson. I swore he did that just to make me blush again. He was so aggravating.

"Happy birthday, Lexi," Ethan said with humor in his voice, and then he bid his farewell to my parents before Mom closed the door behind him.

Dad looked at me quizzically, and Mom smiled, shaking her head.

"What was that all about?" Dad asked.

"It's nothing, dear," Mom said in my defense.

"Nothing my ass. Alexa, he is too old for you," Dad quipped.

"What the hell? I didn't do or say anything." I shot him an embarrassed look, hoping he didn't think back to my very audible sigh earlier.

"Joseph, Lexi knows Ethan is too old. There is nothing to worry about," Mom told him reassuringly.

"Humph," Dad grunted. "Did you find it odd that they didn't want to answer the question if they had any other children?" he asked Mom.

"That was kind of strange. Maybe it's a sore subject, like she couldn't have any more," Mom said with sadness in her voice, as she was remembering that she could never bear a child of her own.

"You're probably right, honey. I'm going to bed. We all have busy days tomorrow."

"Good night, Mom. Good night, Dad." I kissed both of them on the cheek and headed back to my room.

After I was dressed for bed in my pj's, I went out to my balcony before I crawled into bed and sent Devin a quick text to see if he was still awake.

Me: You up?

Devin: Yeah. What's up?

Me: Just met my annoying neighbor. He's a total DB.

Devin: Already making friends?

Me: Not even! He's an ass!

Devin: Sux 2 B U.

Me: Thx jerk!

Devin: Hey. I gotta go. I have last minute homework.

Me: Can I ask u something 1st

Devin: What?

Me: R U mad @ me?

Devin: No.

Me: Thx 4 the clarification >:/

Devin: Anytime

Me: Nite Dev.

Devin: Bye Lexi

Bye, Lexi. What the hell was going on with him? This was really starting to piss me off. First, he cut our text chat short earlier today, and now Devin was just being rude. This birthday sucked. Well, except the part about building a car with my dad. That part was pretty badass.

Having to deal with hottie Ethan and his arrogant ways wasn't helping my mood either. I glanced over at the house of my new friend, and I saw someone sitting at the window again, looking out. I could only assume it was Ethan. That was unless the Gages did have another kid that they kept hidden away for some reason. I shook my head and turned to go back inside when I heard a voice in the distance say, "Good night, Lexi."

I didn't even glance back. I just went into my room, closed the French doors, turned off the lights, and crawled into bed. This really had been a sucky birthday.

# Chapter Two

It's a sunny October morning, and I'm finally sixteen. Being that today is a Saturday, I had to schedule my driving test to get my license on Monday. Since next Friday all the schools are off for some teacher workshop, Devin, my longtime best friend, is driving over to celebrate my birthday with me and my two best girlfriends, Jessa and Becca Ritchfield. They are identical twin sisters. When I met them in junior high, we immediately hit it off and became inseparable. Being around them all the time, I finally began to slowly transform back into a girlie girl, with only a twist of tomboy still left in me.

Both girls are five feet five and have straight, naturally blond hair; hazel eyes; and gymnasts' bodies thanks to our dance and gymnastics classes. Jessa, who is the oldest of the twins by four minutes, keeps her hair short in a pixie style while Becca keeps her hair in long layers. Their hairstyles help people who don't know them tell them apart. When we first met, they told me they stopped playing the switching game on people once they reached junior high because it was too childish. I agreed, although at the time, I secretly thought it would still be fun to prank people.

I think the girls are almost as excited to see Devin as I am, since I strongly believe they are both secretly crushing on him but won't admit it. If he wasn't like a brother to me, I probably would be crushing on him too. What isn't there to like about Devin? He's the varsity quarterback, even though he's only a sophomore. He is definitely swoon-worthy in the looks department, with his six-foot athletic, muscular build. His long blond hair curls just above his eyebrows, and the bedhead look works for him. He has a strong, chiseled jawline, and although his nose is slightly crooked from when he broke it playing street hockey, it doesn't take away from his handsome face. Devin's thick eyelashes only enhance his mesmerizing deep Caribbean-blue eyes. He's all of that, and you throw funny, smart, and charming into the mix and he really is the whole package.

My phone chimes from my nightstand, indicating a text. I glance at the screen and see that it's Devin. He must be sensing that I was just thinking about him.

Devin: Happy 16th Lexi!
Me: Thx Dev! I can't wait 2 c u Fri!
Devin: Same here. What's the plan?
Me: Go-kart racing in Burlingame then back here to swim & watch scary movies with Becca & Jessa.
Devin: Oh. It's not just us?
Me: No. Is that a prob?
Devin: Nah. It's ur day.
Me: Cool. I gotta go downstairs so mom & dad can wish me a happy b-day. C u soon!
Devin: Later

I'm so glad that whatever was up Devin's ass when I first moved to Hillsborough has since been removed. Things were weird the first year, but then we found our long-distance best friend groove, and it got better. Now that he can drive, and soon I can too, I hope we will be almost back to normal.

I head downstairs, and as with every birthday, Mom and Dad greet me with a boisterous "Happy Birthday, Alexa!" when I walk into the kitchen. I really didn't want to make a big deal out of today since I wasn't able to get my license until Monday, so I decided to hold off on my actual celebration until Friday when Devin could partake. My parents were fine with the normal birthday breakfast and then possibly going out to dinner tonight. I'm thankful they are so easygoing and don't need to throw me some huge sweet sixteen shindig to celebrate.

⌒☉

Between going to the movies with Jessa and Becca on my actual birthday and working on building my dad's dream car with him, the weekend flew by, and it's finally Monday, my driving test day. I'm excited and scared at the same time. I head to my bathroom to shower and get ready for school. As soon as I'm ready for my big day, I head downstairs to the kitchen, and I'm greeted with big smiles from my parents. God, I love them. They are both ready for work but want to be sure to see me before school.

"Today's the day, Alexa. I will pick you up from school at three thirty and take you to the DMV to take your driving test," Dad tells me.

"Thanks, Dad. I know it's hard for you to get away from work, and I really appreciate it."

"My only daughter turns sixteen only once. Work can wait," he says with a smile.

"I think I'm more excited for you to get your license than you are," Mom says as she kisses me on the cheek and gives me one of her big hugs.

"I highly doubt that, Mom," I say, hugging her back.

A horn sounds outside, and I know my ride is here.

"You better get out there before Jessa or Becca angers our neighbors with their early morning honking," Mom says laughingly.

"Love you guys!"

"Love you, princess."

"Love you, Lexi."

I sling my backpack over my shoulder as I head out of the house to see Jessa and Becca waiting for me.

"Morning, bitch! Now hurry up!" Jessa yells.

"Shut up! My parents are still inside."

Totally ignoring what I just said about my parents still being home, Becca yells, "Yeah! Hurry up, skank!"

"You two are killing me! I won't let you hang out with me and Dev on Friday if you keep this shit up," I try to say in a stern whisper of a voice, but it falters when I look over at my neighbors' house to see Ethan's sexy-as-hell black Audi R8, which was his high school graduation present. When did he get home?

Both girls look over their shoulders to see what stopped me dead in my tracks, and then both look back at me with big cheesy grins on their faces.

"Your college boy is home, I see," Jessa says teasingly.

"He's not mine, J, so shut your hole."

"Yeah, Jess, she only wishes he was hers," Becca teases.

"Seriously, you two, you're picking today to be total bitches?"

"It's all out of love for ya, girl!" Jessa says.

"Well, screw your love." I pout.

Both girls get back in their car laughing. Just as I go to get into the backseat, I hear a window slide open, and I instantly look up at Ethan's window. He leans out and calls down, "Happy belated birthday, Lexi," in his way-too-sexy voice. On cue, I blush, and only hope to God he didn't hear the banter between me and my friends.

"Thanks, Ethan!" I call up to him. OK, that was a little weird and a whole lot embarrassing. I slide in the backseat, and both girls turn to gawk at me.

"What? He just said happy birthday. Since when's that a crime?"

Jessa laughs. "Since college boy must be crushing on one sophomore in high school."

"Now you're being ridiculous. Drive, woman, or we will be late for school."

"He's smoking hot with those gorgeous gray eyes that would melt panties off any girl. I'm sure he has plenty of college girls vying for his attention, so why would he want a high school girl?" Becca says.

I don't know why it bothers me when Becca says that, especially when I know it's true, but just the mere thought of other girls wanting him and having him really gets under my skin. I have watched him, from afar, bring home girl after girl all through his high school days and even a couple since he's been in college. Never the same girl twice, either.

Regardless, I think he was deliberately trying to drive me crazy the numerous times he would be making out right in front of his house, as if he wanted me to watch. I would glance out my French doors and see a car parked out on the street with the windows fogged up from whatever heady make-out session was taking place inside.

His last conquest is one I won't ever forget. I was sitting out on my balcony doing homework when they drove up. Apparently, she didn't want to keep to the privacy inside of her car. Once Ethan was out of the passenger side, the blonde rounded her car like a lioness after her prey. She shoved Ethan against the passenger door, pinning him there with her waif-like body as she attacked him. Her mouth ravaged him from his earlobes to his neck to his perfect mouth and anywhere else she could latch onto his body. She had no shame as her hand slid down his torso and disappeared into the front of his jeans, moving up and down the length of the erection that I'm sure he had. The entire time she was molesting him out on the street, his eyes were locked on me. I was held captive by the way his gray eyes kept me immobilized in my chair. Ethan kept his hands in his pockets, not once returning her touch or kisses. He let her continue her assault as if he was trying to make me jealous, and sadly, it worked. I was most definitely jealous. All I could do was sit there and wish I was the blonde who got to kiss his perfect lips and feel his masculine body under my fingertips.

"Earth to Lexi. Do you want to stop at Starbucks?" Becca asks, pulling me from my unwelcome thoughts of Ethan.

I glance at my watch. "Yeah. Sure. We have time."

⤸

Dad is waiting out by the curb for me when school lets out. He has a big smile on his face when he asks, "Are you ready for independence?"

"Yep. Let's do this," I say cheerfully.

"Let's hit the road to the DMV, then."

Minutes later, we pull into the DMV parking lot, and I'm surprised to see my mom there too.

"What's Mom doing here? I thought she had a big meeting that couldn't be moved," I ask.

"You are her big meeting. We wanted to surprise you."

We get out of my dad's Audi A7 and walk over to my mom. She has an even bigger smile on her face than my dad did when he picked me up from school.

"Hi, Mom. What are you doing here?"

"I came to wish you luck and give you these." She keeps smiling as she dangles a set of keys in her hand.

Confused, I ask, "What are those?"

"Those are keys to your new but slightly used Audi A3. It's the red one right there," my dad says, pointing to a sleek red Audi A3 hatchback in the first stall.

I scream with joy, "Oh my God! Are you kidding me? This is freaking awesome!" I keep jumping up and down, drawing lots of attention.

"Let's get you checked in so you can get your license and drive your new car home," Dad says.

⟡

An hour later, I'm driving my new car home from the DMV all by myself. I take a longer route just so I can keep enjoying the car and my freedom. Dad mentioned the HomeLink was already connected to our garage, so I can park inside when I get home.

I finally pull up to the house but decide to park outside. I want to take a picture and send it to Devin. I know I will see him Friday, but I am way too excited. When I get out of my car, I see Ethan, as he was just going to get into his R8.

"Nice wheels, Lexi," he says.

"Thanks, Ethan. Yours are still sexier." I say the last part without even thinking and immediately turn the color of my car.

"So you think my car is sexy?" he asks with the arrogant smirk he gets when he knows he's getting to me.

"You know your car is sexy. You don't need me to confirm it," I banter back to him.

"I'm glad you think she's sexy, Lexi. Maybe now that you have your license, I will let you try her out sometime," he says with confidence, or maybe it's arrogance.

"I don't know how to drive a stick," I say a little too breathily.

"Oh, doll, I can most definitely teach you how to drive a stick." His gaze is dark and dangerous.

What the hell is going on here? Is he flirting with me? I'm in high school, for fuck's sake. But damn, this is fun. I didn't even think I knew how to flirt, if that is even what I'm doing.

His last remark has me speechless, and I don't have a witty comeback, so I just smile. At that moment, my parents are just coming down the street. I'm saved by the parental units from this awkward moment.

"See you later, Lexi."

"Bye, Ethan."

My parents pull into the garage and come see why I haven't parked inside yet.

"Is everything OK, Lexi?" Mom asks.

"Yeah. I wanted to take a picture of my new car to send to Dev, and then Ethan was just congratulating me."

"Oh, OK. Well, we stopped and got your favorite Chinese food for dinner. We hope that's all right for your birthday dinner. We both have work to catch up on since we took the afternoon off to surprise you," Dad says.

"That's perfect. I have a lot of homework to do anyway. All these college prep classes are kicking my butt. It's getting harder maintaining my 4.0 GPA," I say honestly.

"Let us know if you need any help. That's what we're here for, princess."

"Thanks. I will see you guys inside in a few minutes."

# Chapter Three

The week seemed to drag by, but it's finally Friday morning, and I just heard the garage door close, indicating my parents have left for work. I don't have school today, and I'm excited that Devin will be here in a couple of hours. I told Jessa and Becca that I will text them when we get back from go-kart racing so we can swim and watch scary movies. I figured this way gives me time to hang out with just Devin. Plus, go-kart racing is not something the twins would enjoy anyway.

I get up out of bed, go brush my teeth, run downstairs to grab a sugar-free Red Bull from the refrigerator, and come back up to my room to sit out on my balcony, as I do most mornings that I don't have school. I grab my laptop to check Facebook, Twitter, and my e-mails. Out of habit, I glance down and see Ethan's car in his driveway. He must be taking some time off if he's still home right now. I'm not sure why he would when he should be close to graduating college.

As I'm scrolling through Facebook and liking random pages and pictures, I hear the front door to Ethan's house open and see a leggy blonde leaving with her heels in hand, doing the walk of shame. Ethan has his arms stretched above his head with his hands placed on the doorjamb, showing off his tight washboard abs and the sexy V where his sweats hang low on his hips. All I could think is, Yum. The blonde turns to kiss him, but just as she tries, he turns his head so she ends up kissing his cheek instead of his lips. All the while, his eyes are fixated on me. A ping of embarrassment followed by jealousy washes through me as I watch this soap opera unfold.

The blonde yells, "Call me!" over her shoulder as she walks down the driveway to her car, which is parked on the street. I swear I hear Ethan laugh a "hell, no" kind of laugh. Soon, the blonde is driving away in her perfectly suited Porsche Boxter.

Ethan is still standing in his doorway, now with his arms crossed over his chest when he acknowledges me in his luscious voice, which makes my toes curl. "Good morning, Lexi."

"I'm sure it is, Ethan," I snap back. My voice sounds a little too irritated for my liking. I don't want him to think the blonde bothers me, even though she most certainly does.

"I'll see you later, Lexi," he says, smirking as he turns to go into his house.

He is so frustrating, but even with that being said, watching his last conquest leave made me wish I was the one doing the walk of shame instead of her. Oh, who am I kidding? I'm a sophomore in high school who has kissed one boy in my entire sixteen years of existence. It was a horrible first kiss, too. It was one that scared me enough to not want to do it again anytime soon.

I was at Becca and Jessa's fourteenth birthday party, and of course everyone decided to play spin the bottle. I was nervous since I'd never played nor had any desire to kiss a guy—that is, until Ethan. It was my turn to spin, and it landed on a boy named Anthony. I was thankful Anthony was cute, which helped ebb my nerves a little bit, but him being cute was all he had going for him. Before I knew what was happening, he had grabbed my face and darted his tongue into my mouth like a lizard. He opened his mouth wider, and as he tried to coax mine to open wider, it felt like he was trying to swallow my whole face. It was the most horrifying and disgusting thing ever. I didn't know if he was jokingly kissing me like that or if he really was that bad. I didn't stick around to ask.

I know I will never get the chance to be with Ethan. I'm the awkward girl next door. Not to mention the fact that I'm a brunette, and he most definitely prefers blondes. The only way I get to be with him is in my very vivid dreams, like the one I had last night. I dreamed of his beautiful gray eyes staring down at me right before he leans in to brush a soft kiss on my pouty lips, followed by trails of smaller kisses over my jawline and down my neck. I moan at this simple show of affection. He holds his weight off of me with one elbow to one side of my head as his free hand teases the hem of my shirt, and I feel the soft brush of his dexterous fingers on the flesh of my stomach. His touch sends an electric shock through my entire body. Just as his hand slides up to cup my needy breast, his mouth covers mine, devouring me with the most sensual kiss as his tongue invades my mouth with urgency. I have one hand resting on his muscular chest, and the other is holding his head to me as I deepen the kiss. I can feel his arousal rubbing against my thigh. And every time my hand that was once on his chest starts to move down his rock-hard body toward his erection, I wake up, and I'm left feeling extremely aroused with an ache deep in my core and a wet sensation between my thighs. I ask myself the same frustrating question every time: Why can't I get further in my dreams of him? Oh, I know why. Because I wouldn't know what to do if I did go further!

It's been an hour since I came out to my balcony, and I don't even realize so much time had passed since my mind drifted to my most recent dream of Ethan. I'm startled when my phone chimes with a text from Devin.

Devin: Lvg now
Me: Yay! C U soon.

I shake off my thoughts of Ethan and go inside to shower and get ready for my birthday celebration with my best friend.

⟳

I hear the engine of Devin's '68 Chevelle rumbling down the street. I check my makeup one last time; grab a hair tie, my wallet, and a sweatshirt; and bolt out of my room, down the stairs, and out the front door.

Devin is just now approaching the bottom of the stairs when I fly down them and jump into his arms to give him a big hug. He almost loses his balance at my force but keeps us both vertical. His bulging arms wrap around me a little tighter than normal, but I think nothing of it.

"God, I've missed you," I say after he puts me down.

"I've missed you too," he says sweetly. "Look at you, all grown up with a driver's license now."

"Yeah, I know. I'm a complete package now that I have some freedom." I laugh jokingly.

"You have always been a complete package, Lex."

I tilt my head to the side, trying to comprehend what that was supposed to mean, when all of a sudden, my breath catches and heart skips a beat. My eyes widen, as my attention is now focused on Ethan approaching us. I quickly glance back up to Devin's face as he turns his head to see what I'm looking at and releases his hold. I swear I hear Devin say, "Fuck," under his breath, but I choose to ignore it since my mind is reeling as to why Ethan is walking over here.

"Hi, Lexi," Ethan says in a cool voice that sends chills down my spine.

"Hi, Ethan," I say, flustered. "Um, this is my best friend, Devin." I don't know why I felt the need to explain that Devin is just a friend, but it is out of my mouth before I know it.

"Devin, this is Ethan, my neighbor."

"I know who he is, Lexi," Devin says with slight irritation.

Both guys just stand there staring each other down. What the hell is going on here? For being outside, I feel like I'm being suffocated by too much testosterone.

It seems like forever goes by before Devin finally reaches out to shake Ethan's hand.

"Ethan," Devin says as they shake hands.

When the handshake ends, Ethan looks over at me with a look in his eyes that I don't recognize. Usually, he has that smug smirk on his face when he knows he's getting under my skin.

"Where're you headed to, Lexi?" he asks.

His question catches me off guard since he's never cared where I was going before this moment. Just then, as if a light bulb clicks inside my mind, it dawns on me that he's never cared before this moment because now there is another extremely handsome male standing beside me. Was that a hint of jealousy I saw flash in his eyes after the handshake? Oh, stop it, Lexi. Get your head out of your ass. You are reading way too much into this.

"Um, we're headed to GoKart Racer in Burlingame," I finally answer. I feel my cheeks heating up and the sudden need to get out of this close proximity to Ethan. He makes my body react in strange ways even when he's not this close, and right now, these feelings are heightened because he's close enough to touch, to feel. And God only knows I do want to touch him.

"Let's go, Lex," Devin says curtly as he grabs my hand to lead me toward his car. The sudden contact with Devin brings me back to the present situation. I cannot figure out where Devin's hostility toward Ethan is coming from.

"O-O-OK," I stutter out.

"I'll be seeing you later, Lexi," Ethan says with a wink.

That's the second time today he's said those promising words, and the wink completely throws me off balance so that I have a slight misstep. "See ya," I say over my shoulder as Devin tows me to his car.

That was just the strangest—I don't even know what to call it.

Once we are in the car, I turn to Devin and ask, "Dev, what was that all about?"

"What?" he says, sounding annoyed.

"That so-called pissing match back there. Ethan is my neighbor and was just being friendly."

"Friendly? Ha! He was trying to stake some sort of claim on you before you said I was your 'friend.' How could you not see that?"

"You are so wrong, Dev!" I shout. "He's in college, for goodness sake!"

"College or not, he wants you, and I'm not OK with that, Lexi."

"You're being ridiculous, so drop it. This is not a conversation I want to have with you. Let's just go have fun, OK?"

"Sure. Whatever."

What in the hell is going on with my best friend?

I've sent a text to Becca and Jessa to let them know we are on our way back to my house from Burlingame. Once we finally got to GoKart Racer, Devin seemed to lighten up, and we had a really great time racing. I won two races and he won one, but I think he let me win the last one because, after all, we were there celebrating my birthday. Of course, being the friend he is, he would never admit to throwing the race.

When we turn down my street, I'm actually glad that I don't see the R8 in Ethan's driveway. I don't need any more awkward moments today.

By the time we park, Jessa and Becca are driving down the street. I stop to wait for them before heading into the house.

"Hey, bitch," Becca says as she's getting out of the car.

"Hey, skank," I tease back.

"Hi, Devin," Jessa says with a purr to her voice and a bat of her lashes at my best friend.

I just shake my head and roll my eyes.

"Jessa, Becca. It's always nice to see you two," he says with a cocky smile that seems so foreign to me. Devin has never exuded arrogance, and right now that is the only vibe I get from him.

"Well, are we swimming or what? I have a new bikini that I'm just dying to get wet," Becca says, flirting with Devin.

"Oh my God, you two! Leave Dev alone!" I laugh. "Come on. Maybe the cold water will cool you both down a notch or twenty."

We all swim awhile and hang out in the hot tub. It's pure entertainment watching Becca and Jessa vying for Devin's attention, but his attention always comes back to me. I conclude that it's the fact that I'm his best friend and he came across the bay to see me for my birthday, so of course his attention will be mainly focused on me.

After we all have pruned from our afternoon submerged in water and then rinsed off and changed back into our clothes, we all sit downstairs in the family room getting ready to watch a marathon of Friday the 13th movies when we hear Becca's phone go off with the ringtone of "The Imperial March" from Star Wars.

"Hey, Dad," she says. "What? Right now? We were just going to watch a movie. OK, OK. Fine, we'll be home in ten," she says and then ends the call.

"We gotta go, Jess. Dad said Grandma is there for a surprise visit, and you know how she gets if we aren't around."

"You're kidding, right?" Jess says in annoyance.

"Nope. Let's go. Sorry, Lexi, for cutting this short," Becca apologizes to me. Then she turns to Devin. "I hope to see you sooner than later, Devin."

"Yeah, Devin, see you soon," Jess chimes in with a wink for good measure.

"Later, girls," Devin says with that cute smile he gets when he's slightly embarrassed.

Now that the twins are gone and it's just Devin and I alone on the couch, everything feels awkward. I can't quite put my finger on why it feels different sitting here with him when we've done this a million times before. We always watched movies together, and this wasn't any different, yet there's something about Devin that is definitely not the same.

"Sorry about J and Becs," I say to break the uncomfortable silence.

"Sorry for what? They're cute."

"OK, well, in that case, I'm not sorry then," I say with a smile.

I press play on the remote to the Blu-ray player and the beginning credits of Friday the 13th starts. We sit side by side for a while as the movie plays. It's popcorn time, so I get up to go make us some Jiffy Pop in the kitchen. As I'm standing by the stove, moving the handle back and forth vigorously as the directions say to, Devin comes up behind me and rests his hands on my hips. The way he grabs me and the feel of his muscular body behind me send a shock wave through my body that I have never experienced when he's touched me before. Then again, Devin has never touched me in such an intimate way.

"That smells good," he says as he leans over my shoulder, his breath warm by my ear.

"Well, duh. It's our staple popcorn for marathon movie watching," I say in an effort to not sound affected by his close proximity and where his hands flex at my hips.

I'm not exactly sure how it happens, because it happens so quickly, but one second I'm making popcorn, and the next second I'm spun around, Jiffy Pop flying out of my hand, and I'm in Devin's arms, held tight against his body. His left hand fists into my hair at the nape of my neck as his right hand presses firmly at the small of my back. His lips smash into mine as he tries to coax them to part with subtle licks of his tongue. My lips concede and part slightly. The tip of his soft tongue swiftly touches mine, taking advantage of my invite. For a brief moment, I actually find myself lost in his kiss. Because my first kiss was horrendous, I find myself enjoying Devin's. His full lips are soft, his mouth is warm, and our tongues move effortlessly together. The hand that Devin had at the small of my back slides lower, resting on my backside. I can feel his erection pressing against my stomach. Just as his mouth leaves mine to trail light kisses down my neck, my mind snaps back to reality, and that reality is that I'm making out with my best friend.

I shove Devin back a step. "What in the hell are you doing, Dev?" My voice is shaky.

"What does it look like, Lexi? I'm kissing you because I like you. I've always liked you. You're beautiful, funny, and smart. We're good together. I figured if there was any time to see if we have something more than friendship, that time was right now," he answers unapologetically.

"How can you do this to me, to our friendship?" I'm near tears at this point.

"You just kissed me back, Lex! You can't deny you felt something more in that one kiss," he snaps.

"Dev, you're my best friend. Of course I'm going to feel something. Please don't ruin this for us," I plead.

"Ruin us? I'm trying to make us better!" He's shouting now as anger vibrates off his tensed body.

"Devin, I—"

"Stop, Lexi! Just stop. I get it. You would rather have Mr. Joe College next door," he says, sounding defeated.

"Wait...what? Where in the hell is that coming from? He has nothing to do with what just freaking happened here." I'm completely shaking at this point. My vision is blurred from the tears that are now trickling down my flushed cheeks.

"I saw the way you looked at him today. I've only dreamed of having you look at me that way. I had to kiss you, Lexi. I had to at least try," he says, before he turns to leave.

Time is standing still as I bring my fingers to my lips, swollen from Devin's passionate kiss. My thoughts are scattered. I'm trying to think of what to say to save this friendship, but nothing is coming to mind. I hear his car start, snapping me from my thoughts. My feet finally move as I run out the front door, yelling, "Devin, stop! Wait, dammit!" But I'm too late. He can't hear me over the roar of his engine, and I'm sure he's not looking in the rearview mirror to see me standing there.

What the fuck just happened? Why did Devin do this? I'm really beginning to loathe my birthdays. I'm crying tears of devastation, knowing I just lost my best friend. I sit down on the bottom stair, putting my elbows on my knees and holding my head in my hands as I sob uncontrollably. I must be crying really hard not to hear Ethan's car drive down the street or hear him walk up and crouch down right in front of me.

"Lexi, are you OK?" Ethan asks cautiously, using his index finger to lift my chin so I look at him.

"Do I look OK?" I snap back, turning my head, trying to avoid looking at him, not even caring how I must look to the gorgeous man in front of me.

"Did he hurt you?"

"Why do you care?" I squeak out between sobs.

"I'll go after him if he hurt you, Lexi. So I'm asking again, did he hurt you?"

Shrugging my shoulders, I answer, "Yes, he hurt me, but not the way you're probably thinking." I stand, wiping my nose with the back of my hand, which is very unladylike. "I'm gonna go inside."

He reaches out and grabs my shoulder to stop me. I turn as he asks, "See you later, Lexi?" It's a question this time, instead of a statement of fact.

"Yeah," is all I can manage as I turn to head back into the house.

Once I'm inside, I head back to the kitchen, realizing the burner is still on. I shut it off and start to clean up the popcorn when I just fall back against the cabinet, sitting on the floor, putting my face in my hands, and begin to cry all over again.

I'm not sure how long I've been sitting there on the kitchen floor crying, but I hear the garage door raising, signaling my parents are home. I am in no mood to try to explain why I'm a bawling mess, since I'm still unsure of what exactly happened today to even give an explanation. I hurry to my feet, throw away the popcorn, and run upstairs to my room.

Moments later, I hear my mom call up to me, "Lexi?"

I try to steady my voice before I answer. "Yeah, Mom?"

"You left the Blu-ray player and TV on with some slasher movie."

"Shit," I say to myself. Louder, I say, "Sorry, Mom. Can you turn it off, please? I just got undressed to take a bath." I lie, which is rare for me.

"Sure. Are you hungry? I was going to make spaghetti and meatballs for dinner."

"No, thanks. I had a late lunch with Dev...in." I barely croak out his name and pray my mom doesn't catch it.

"OK, sweetheart. How is Devin?" she asks.

My voice is barely audible when I say to myself, "Oh, he's a mess, and I'm pretty sure he hates me now." But when I think I can answer her, I just yell down, "He's fine," and shut my bedroom doors.

As I start to fill my bathtub, I grab my cell phone and, with my hands still shaking, send Devin a text.

**Me: We REALLY need to talk Dev. Please call me.**

I wait five minutes and still have no reply. He probably isn't home yet. I strip out of my clothes and slide into my bubble bath. I'm replaying the events of today through my head over and over again. First, there was Devin and Ethan's weird, testosterone-filled pissing match. Then Devin was ignoring the twins' excessive flirting, and then Devin's mouth on mine with the kiss that will forever change our relationship. Damn him!

Then my thoughts drift back to Ethan, crouching in front of me after my failed attempt at stopping Devin from leaving. Ethan looking male model gorgeous while I sit there looking a hot mess as he offers me comfort and to go kick Devin's ass for hurting me. I guess his big brother tendencies kicked in, because there is positively no other explanation that I can think of.

Seriously, what the hell happened today? Was today "Let's Fuck with Lexi Day"?

I'm starting to prune, so I get out of the tub, dry myself off, and throw on some pajama shorts and a camisole for bed. After I have washed my face, moisturized, and brushed my teeth, I grab my phone, and there is a text message, but it's from Becca.

**Becca: Sry we bailed. Hope ur snuggled with your BFF Devin on the couch.**

Ugh! Why would Becca even type that?

**Me: No worries. Dev went home already.**

Becca: Bummer. If I were you I would have at least made out with him. Well gotta go back to Grams. TTYL
Me: TTYL

Since I haven't heard back from Devin, I try to call him, but his phone goes straight to voice mail. I leave a message.

"Dev. Please call me back. We really need to talk and clear this mess up, OK?" I hit end.

I grab my laptop and bring it out to the balcony with me. I'm just sitting there, lost in thought, when I hear Ethan's window open.

"Feeling any better, Lexi?" he asks.

"Not really."

"My parents are out of town. Do you want to come over and watch a movie with me? It might help take your mind off whatever that was earlier."

I'm staring vacantly across the cul-de-sac at Ethan's window, trying to figure out why he would invite me over. I'm a sixteen-year-old train wreck right now.

If it were yesterday that Ethan asked me to come over, I would have found a way to sneak over there in a heartbeat, but today is a different story. Today has been one fucked-up day that has left my brain very much confused.

"Thanks, but not tonight. It's been a rough day."

"The offer is always open," he says sweetly.

"Thanks, Ethan." I hear his window close.

I open up my laptop, and staring back at me is my background picture of Devin and me laughing on the beach in Maui from one of our family vacations. The pain in my chest gets tighter, and I want to start crying again, but the tears won't fall.

I click open my e-mails, and there is a new message from Devin from a half hour ago. I shakily click read.

Alexa~

I'm not sorry for kissing you. I've wanted to for so long. I probably would have by now if you hadn't moved away. You are everything I want, but I now know I can't have. I'm not sure how this
friendship can continue to work when I'm in love with you and
you are obviously infatuated with someone else. I think it would
be best if we didn't talk to each other for a while, or at least until
the pain subsides for both of us. I really hope someday we will
get past this, but right now it just hurts too much. I love you, Lexi,
always.

Love,
D.

The tears I couldn't shed just moments ago are falling freely now. I
slam my laptop shut, go back inside, crawl into my bed, and cry into
my pillow until I fall asleep.

# Chapter Four

After days of moping around, I eventually told my mom and the twins what had happened that day with Devin. Mom hugged me tightly and assured me that things would work out in time, and I just needed to have patience and give Devin the space he asked for. The twins weren't surprised that Devin had feelings for me, but they were surprised that I didn't have those same feelings toward him. It took a couple of weeks before they finally stopped asking about him and like the best friends they are, kept me busy.

I waited a few months before I tried to call, text, or even e-mail Devin, but I never got a reply back. I even drove to his house, but his dad, George, said he was out with his buddies. I knew he was lying because Devin's car was in the driveway and I saw him peeking out from the blinds in his bedroom. I smiled weakly at George and asked him to have Devin call me. He never did.

It's been two years and four days since I received that last e-mail from my ex–best friend. It has also been two years and four days since I had my last kiss. Not having Devin in my life still hurts just as much today as it did the day everything went to shit. Not to mention Ethan is barely around anymore. After he took that semester off, his parents told him he had two years to finish getting his real estate law degree or they were cutting him off.

After all that had happened with Devin, I just buried myself in my schoolwork and figured it was the best thing for me. I maintained my 4.0 GPA in all of my advanced college prep classes, was head cheerleader, and was captain of the girl's gymnastics team at my school. I also kept busy with non-school-related activities as well, since my dad suggested it would help with my college applications. I volunteered my time at the animal shelter a couple days a week as well as an after-school program for underprivileged kids in San Mateo. I enjoy tutoring and being someone the kids can look up to and talk to if they feel the need. Helping these kids is the reason I want to major in psychology. I want to make a difference in someone's life.

As always, Dad was right about my grades, school, and non-school-related activities when it came to my college applications. I only applied to three colleges, hoping one of them would want me—Washington University, UCLA, and Stanford, which was my number one college of choice since I loved the peninsula and really didn't want to leave.

It's a nice day out, and I am detailing my little red Audi A3 when the mailman hands me the mail. I thank him and quickly look to see if anything is for me, and sure enough, there is a large envelope from Stanford University addressed to me between engineering and architecture magazines. I throw the rest of the mail on my passenger seat and proceed to tear open my envelope. I hold my breath as I take out the contents. A sigh of relief escapes my lips and a huge grin spreads across my face as I stand there, reading my early acceptance letter from Stanford, where I will study psychology.

After jumping around in circles, excited and completely forgetting everything that has happened between me and Devin, my kneejerk reaction is to immediately text him.

Me: I got into Stanford!

I don't know why I think today will be different than all the other days he never responded. I stand waiting, hopeful that today will be the day he will end the silence. I'm kidding myself. Devin never responds.

With my car radio blasting Tiesto's "Red Lights" from my iPod, I continue to clean my car. House music gives me that kick of energy when I listen to it. Since it's still a warm October day, I'm wearing flip-flops with white shorts that show off my long, tan, and toned legs and a camisole tank top that accents my perky 34C breasts. My hair is a naturally lighter brown now from the summer sun, and I have it up in a messy bun to keep it out of my face while I tend to my car. I'm bent over with my head in my car, vacuuming the floor, when I feel a hand grab my hip from behind. All at once I jump, smacking my head on the doorjamb and dropping the vacuum hose as a scream escapes my mouth. I turn around, ready to punch whoever is behind me.

I'm stopped short as his hand grabs my wrist, pulling me to his hard body before I can connect the punch. His stormy gray eyes penetrate my honey-colored eyes with molten desire. A desire for me? That, I don't know. My brain isn't functioning properly being in his arms.

My breathing teeters, and his name is a whisper. "Ethan."

"Happy belated eighteenth birthday, Lexi," he says in a tone that sends an electric shock straight to my core as he leans down to turn off the shop vac. His eyes come back to mine. "How's your head?" he asks with a cocked eyebrow and reaches to rub the back of my head where I'm sure there is a knot forming. His gaze drifts from my eyes down to my lips, then to my heaving chest, as I'm still trying to breathe.

Catching my breath seems to be a difficult task since I am being held firmly against Ethan's hard chest. His cologne is intoxicating, making him smell delicious, and it's playing with my senses. He licks his lips as he brings his gaze back to my eyes and releases his hold. My knees are weak when he releases me, and he immediately grabs me back around the waist before I drop to the ground. He waits a few moments, until he knows for certain my balance is steady, before letting me go.

My brain finally kicks in. "I d-d-didn't hear you drive up," I stutter. It's all I can get out of my mouth.

"How could you with your music blasting and the vacuum running?" he teases. "I must say, though, the sight of you bent over shaking that fine ass of yours while vacuuming is one I won't forget anytime soon," he says with his ever-present arrogant smirk he gets when he knows he's affected me.

My cheeks heat with his last comment. I draw in my bottom lip with my teeth, trying to conjure some witty comeback, but the way those gray eyes are staring at me, undressing me, leaves me completely speechless. If one didn't know any better, one would think Ethan was talking to a mute since I am lacking any kind of vocabulary at this particular moment.

I'm not sure how long we stand there staring at one another until we are literally shaken out of our trance when the earth moves below our feet. Ethan instinctively grabs my hand, pulling me toward my garage. Once we are inside, safe in the doorjamb leading from the garage into the house, he just holds me close as the earthquake rocks through our neighborhood. Things are falling off the shelving in the garage, and I can hear glass crashing to the floor inside the house from the violent tremors that shake my house.

In this moment, I remember back to when I was a freshman and we read about an earthquake that devastated the Bay Area back in the late eighties, and here we are again, just days past the twenty-fourth anniversary of that particular earthquake and we are getting rocked by another vicious quake.

Once the initial shaking has subsided and we are only feeling trembles of aftershocks, Ethan looks down into my eyes, grabs my face in his hands, and crushes his warm, soft lips to mine. My eyes flutter closed as his tongue dances over my lips, begging to be let into my mouth. I wrap my arms around his waist and give in to what he wants, what I have dreamed of for so long. I cannot believe I am in the arms of Ethan Gage, and he is kissing me—devouring me is more like it.

He breaks the kiss, leaving us both breathless and panting, and looks warily into my eyes. "Are you OK?"

Dazed and shocked from the kiss, I answer, "Yeah, I think so. Thank you for bringing me to safety."

"You don't have to thank me. I'm glad I was here to protect you," he says as he leans down, placing a featherlight kiss on my lips.

"I should get my car inside and grab my cell phone. My parents are probably freaking out. They went across the bay today for a charity golf tournament."

"I'll stay with you until they get home."

"You don't have to, Ethan."

"I wasn't asking. Now go get your car off the street while I pick up the stuff that fell off the shelves in here. We'll check the damage inside together."

"Thank you," I say as I lean in to hug him, just so I can feel his body against mine again. His arms wrap around my shoulders, hugging tightly.

⟳

I've been trying to call my parents for an hour now, but cellular service seems to be out because of the earthquake. I can't get a call or text to go through to anyone. Since coming inside, Ethan and I have cleaned up the glass from a couple of pictures that fell from the walls and my mom's favorite vase. She's going to be upset that her Tiffany crystal vase is now in a million pieces.

"Oh my God! I almost forgot, I need to go check the back garage,"

I say frantically.

"Calm down. Let's go," he says, offering me his hand.

We walk out to the garage that is behind my house. I unlock the side door and step inside. Ethan is right behind me, but he stops when he sees what is in the garage, and I hear him say under his breath, "Fuck me." Then he says in his normal voice, "Damn, that is a nice fucking car. I can see why you were so worried." He admires the almost finished MK4 AC Shelby replica my dad and I have been building over the last few years. All that's left to do is install the 427 Ford motor, put the body on the frame, and then it's off to the auto body shop for the finishing touches. My dad and I decided on blue with white stripes. We wanted to keep it classic and true to the original AC Shelby.

"It's a Factory Five MK4 Roadster, a replica of the '65 AC Shelby Cobra, which also happens to be my dad's dream car," I say proudly. "We're building it together. My mom was supposed to help too, but she just brings my dad beers and me Diet Dr. Pepper or water, and then she will sit over there on that chair in the corner with her wine and read one of her erotic novels she likes while Dad and I work on the car."

"I couldn't picture your mom getting dirty," he says with a smile.

"Yeah, not so much." I smile.

After Ethan admires the car thoroughly and I make sure there is no real damage to the car or the garage, we head back into the house.

I turn the TV on, but it just shows the emergency broadcast symbol. I've tried the radio, but it's hard following the chaos they are reporting. I catch bits and pieces of multiple traffic collisions, downed power lines, structural damage throughout the Bay Area, water line breaks causing flooding, and a multitude of other things. The station seems to be concentrating mainly on one really bad accident on Interstate 580 that has both east- and westbound lanes closed off between Pleasanton and Castro Valley. There is an eighteen-wheeler that flipped from the force of the earthquake and collided with four other vehicles. The reports say there are fatalities as a result of the semi overturning.

I'm getting more anxious as time keeps ticking by and I don't hear from my parents. Knowing they were on the East Bay today has me worrying. I've been pacing back and forth in my family room. Ethan is sitting on my couch, periodically checking his phone for cell service and watching me pace.

"Hey, why don't you come over here and sit with me on the couch before you wear a hole in the hardwood floor with all of your pacing? I know you're worried. Your parents are fine, Lexi. I'm sure once cellular is restored, all of your text messages will get to them and theirs to you."

I smile weakly as I sit next to him on the couch. "I know you're right. I just hate this waiting around. I really do appreciate you being here right now. I would probably be making myself crazy if you weren't."

"I wouldn't want to be any place else right now."

"Can I ask you something without you getting mad?"

"OK," he says warily.

"Why did you kiss me back there? Was it in the heat of the moment?"

"That's an easy question to answer," he says and then continues, "I've wanted to kiss you awhile now. Watching you grow into this incredibly gorgeous woman was not an easy task. I had to wait until you were legal, Lexi, plain and simple. It took everything I had to not kiss you that night you were crying on your doorstep. I wanted to take away the pain you were feeling."

I look at him in shock. He's wanted to kiss me all this time? His admission has me floating on cloud nine right now. But his admission has now made me think of Devin and the fateful kiss that took my best friend from me.

Trying to shake the sadness and unease, I admit shyly, "I've dreamt of kissing you ever since the first day we met."

"I know you have," he says with a wink and his arrogant smirk I've grown to love over the years. It's as if they are only for me.

We are sitting quietly, and I don't know where I find the courage, but the need to feel Ethan's firm body pressed to mine again, his hands on me, lips kissing me, is so intense that I move to straddle him. The look on his face is of surprise when I clumsily swing my leg over his lap, facing him, with my hands resting on his chest. I can feel the flex of his chest muscles react to the touch of my hands. I slowly lean in and lightly brush my lips to his. For once, it's his breath that hitches, and a deep moan escapes the back of his throat. His mouth opens just enough, granting me access, and our tongues meld together, tasting each other, exploring one another's mouths as his hands move to cup my ass, pulling me closer to him. I move my hands from his chest; I lock my fingers behind his neck. I can feel his erection through his jeans. He's hard for me, because of me. This fuels my inner goddess that I didn't know existed, and subconsciously, I start to rock my hips against the bulge in his jeans, trying to alleviate the ache that I now feel between my thighs. My sex is throbbing with the need to be touched. I've only experienced this feeling in my dreams of Ethan. Him hard and pressing against the apex between my thighs makes my core feel like it's on fire and only he can put it out.

Ethan pulls from the kiss, gently holding me back. "Lexi," he murmurs in a throaty tone, "we need to slow it down. I'm barely hanging on here, and I don't want your parents coming home to me buried inside your sweet pussy while you scream my name."

I'm speechless. No one has ever spoken to me that way. Ethan's words hit me hard. As I feel my sex clench tighter, my core is an inferno, and I can feel my arousal on my panties. A shock wave rolls down my spine. I don't want to stop with just kissing. I want Ethan to take me, possess me. I want to completely give myself to him in every way possible.

"I want you, Ethan," I whisper in his ear, licking the lobe lightly. "I've wanted you for so long. Don't stop now," I beg as I gently rock my hips again, trying to lean in to kiss him again.

He holds me back so he can look me in the eyes with heated sincerity. "Believe me, I want to do a whole lot more than kiss that luscious mouth of yours and dry hump you through your clothes, but right now is not the right time."

"You have some serious willpower, Gage. I'm ready to shatter over here."

"I told you, Lexi—I've been waiting a long time for you. I'm not going to ruin it by moving too fast or having your parents walk in."

What the hell? I'm throwing myself at him, and he's denying me. He pulls me back into him for a hug, and I take the opportunity to place open-mouthed kisses along his jawline and down his neck.

"Fuck me. Are you trying to kill me, woman?"

"Kill you, no. Fuck you, yes," I tease.

"My God, you are sexy when you are horny," he growls, kissing my neck.

For a minute, I think I might have him surrendering.

"You're not so bad yourself," I pant between shallow breaths.

The TV makes a funny sound, capturing both our attentions as the screen changes from the emergency broadcast sign to the news, which stops our sexual banter.

There is aerial coverage being shown of the big-rig accident on Interstate 580. A couple of the vehicles involved are completely demolished. You can't even tell what kind of vehicles they were, let alone their color. The anchorman confirms six fatalities, and the only two survivors who were involved were airlifted to Oakland's trauma center and are listed in critical condition.

Whatever desire I recently had coursing through my veins has diminished. I dismount Ethan, taking in the news footage, and idly sit beside him to watch. The anchorman continues to say that the earthquake that just wreaked havoc on the Bay Area registered at a 7.4 magnitude, surpassing the earthquake twenty-four years ago.

I'm shaking now. Silence from my parents is not normal. I grab my cell phone to see if cellular reception has been restored and if any of my text messages have sent. Through blurred vision, I see I have full bars and all messages have sent successfully. I immediately try calling my parents again, and both of their phones go to voice mail. My stomach turns as nausea hits full force, and silent tears trickle down my cheeks.

"Hey. They will call," Ethan says as he wipes away my errant tears and then grabs my hand in an attempt to comfort me.

"Have you tried your parents?"

"They're vacationing in London. I'll call them tomorrow."

"Oh, OK. Do you have any siblings to worry about?" I'm not sure why I asked that question, since it has never been clear whether or not he has a brother or sister. I just remember the awkwardness when my mom asked Olivia if Ethan was her only child.

Ethan gets up from the couch, tension vibrating off of his rigid frame. He goes over to our bar, which spans halfway down the left wall of the family room. I watch as he pours an amber liquid in two tumblers and brings one to me.

"Here. Drink this. It will help your nerves."

"Thanks," I say nervously. I've never had alcohol before. Well, that's not entirely true. One night while my dad and I were working on the car, he let me have a sip of his beer, but it was god-awful so I never had the desire to ever try anything else. Not from their lack of trying, but I never even had the fruity drinks the twins have at parties.

We both shoot back the amber liquid from our glasses. I cough as the liquid burns its way down my throat, but I welcome the feeling. He takes my glass, placing both on the coffee table. Ethan then grabs the blanket on the other end of the couch and brings it over to where I'm sitting. He sits back down, covers us both with the blanket, and wraps his arms around my waist. I nestle my back to his front as we continue to watch the news in silence.

"Why would you ask about a sibling?" Ethan finally says, breaking the silence.

I can feel tension radiate off his body in waves.

"I don't know, Ethan. It's really none of my business if you do or don't have a brother or sister or both."

Ethan doesn't offer any more information on the subject, and I don't push him for answers. It's obvious there is something he and his family are hiding, but it really is none of my business.

After a while of quiet TV watching, I tell him, "I got into Stanford. I found out today."

"That's great," Ethan says, placing a kiss on the back of my head.

"You're the first person I've told. I tried to text Dev—" I stop myself before finishing my sentence.

"What was that?" His voice sounds a little irritated.

"Nothing. It doesn't matter," I say.

"You were going to say you tried to text Devin, weren't you?"

I feel Ethan's body tense just at the mention of Devin. I still don't get their issue with each other. I must really be dumb and naïve when it comes to the male species.

"Like I said, it doesn't matter. He hasn't had any contact with me in over two years."

"What happened that night?"

"What night?" I say nonchalantly.

"Don't play dumb with me, Lex. It's not going to work."

"It really is nothing worth talking about. I can feel your tension just at the mention of his name."

"Well, it must have been something for him to drive away, leaving you crying on your doorstep, and never talk to you again."

I hesitate, deciding whether or not I want to tell him. After a few minutes, I finally concede. "He kissed me, and I kissed him back briefly before I realized what we were doing."

Ethan's body is heated steel against my back.

"Turn and look at me, Lex." His voice is demanding.

I slowly turn in his arms, with one leg bent at the knee between us, and I slide my other leg over his lap so I am now facing him. I don't think I could ever get tired of staring at the man in front of me. His chiseled facial features and liquid gray eyes encased by thick dark eyelashes truly make him beautiful.

"I had a feeling it was something like that when I saw you crying," he admits. "So I take it he was in love with you?"

"I guess so," I say, shrugging. "At least that was what the e-mail said."

"He's a fool for not sticking around and fighting for you."

"Devin was hurt, Ethan. I don't think I would have stuck around either if I was just rejected." My words come out defensively.

"When it's worth fighting for, you fight," he states matter-of-factly.

He takes his free hand and brings it up to the side of my neck, pulling me to his lips. His tongue glides over my pursed lips until I slightly open them. Ethan then takes full advantage; his tongue delves in, invading my mouth once again.

Kissing Ethan is intoxicating and could easily become an addiction. I slowly move my left hand toward his torso. Finding the hem of his shirt, I slide my hand under it so my fingers can caress his bare skin with no barriers. His abs flex at my light touch, and I swear I feel him shiver.

Ethan hisses a single word, "Fuck," as soon as he feels my flesh on his flesh. A quiet moan escapes his lips. I can feel his rigid length getting hard again under the calf of my leg lying across his lap.

"You are a dangerous girl, Alexa."

Hearing him say my given name makes my stomach flutter with butterflies, and I can feel the wetness between my legs. My nipples are hardened peaks that are firmly pressing against my lacy bra, wanting to be teased, touched, and caressed. There is no way to hide how extremely turned on I am. I want this beautiful man naked, sliding his sweaty body over mine as his cock glides in and out of my sex.

"Please, Ethan," I plead. "Take me to my room, and fuck me."

My body freezes after the last words tumble out of my mouth before I have a chance to stop them. Being a virgin, you wouldn't expect those words to be something I would say to the person who will be deflowering me, but there they were, out there, and I couldn't take them back.

He groans, grabbing my wrist and removing my hand from under his shirt. His face looks pained, as if removing my hand physically hurt him.

"Not tonight, but I promise it will be soon. You are a hard woman to resist," he says with a hint of regret in his voice.

"You can't blame me for trying again," I say with a little laugh, trying to lighten his mood.

He moves my leg so he can get up from the couch and grabs our glasses in one swift motion. He pours each of us another drink as my phone chimes. I grab it, hoping it's one of my parents. As I glance at the screen, I'm disappointed to see it's not.

Jessa: Hey girl. U ok?
Me: I'm good. U guys?
Jessa: Fine. That was crazy ass shit!
Me: Yeah it was.
Jessa: Just wanted to chk on u. Dad won't let us lv the house.
ttyl xo

Me: Thx. Xo

"Who was that?" Ethan asks with one eyebrow cocked as he hands me another shot.

"It was Jessa, one of the twins."

"Checking on you?"

"Yeah. She and Becca are good like that."

⌒⌒

I'm not sure what time it is, but I'm startled awake by my doorbell ringing. At first, I think I'm dreaming, but I realize that I am actually lying on the couch with Ethan's arms wrapped around me from behind. We must have fallen asleep after our third—or was it the fourth?—shot because that is the last thing I remember.

I grab my phone from the coffee table and see that it's nearly two o'clock in the morning. I still have no messages or voice mails from my parents. I can feel the color draining from my face, and the nausea is back again full force.

There's a knock at the door, followed by the doorbell ringing again. I get up to answer it. Ethan sits up quickly and runs his hands through his hair and over his face in an attempt to wake up. He's on my heels as we head up to the front door.

"Let me answer it, Lexi," he says with an edge of worry in his voice.

"OK." I step aside, allowing him access to the front door.

Ethan opens the door, and I hear a male voice say, "Good evening, sir. Is this the Morgan household?"

"Yes, it is, Officer." When I hear Ethan say "Officer," I poke my head around his broad shoulder to see the man in uniform on my porch.

"I'm Officer Chavez. Is this your residence, sir?"

I find my voice and move past Ethan into full view of the officer.

"No, Officer Chavez. This is my house. This is my neighbor, Ethan Gage," I say, trying to steady my voice.

"May I come in, miss?" he asks.

"Alexa. My name is Alexa Morgan," I answer, opening the door wider so the officer can step inside. "Has something happened to my parents?" I ask the second he is in my foyer. I've barely closed the front door before the words come out.

"Why don't you have a seat, Miss Morgan?"

My body is already trembling as Ethan grabs my hand and leads me into the living room off the foyer. We sit down on the couch my parents and I sat on the day I met Ethan as Officer Chavez sits across from us with a mournful look in his eyes.

"Miss Morgan, have you been watching the news since the earthquake?"

"Y-y-yes," I stutter. I can feel a chill start to run through my veins. A roaring sound is in my ears, and I don't want to hear what this man in front of me has to tell me. Ethan's grip on my hand gets tighter, and his thumb is rubbing back and forth across the top, silently trying to comfort me and calm my shaking body.

Officer Chavez continues, "I'm sorry to be the one to inform you, but your parents were involved in the accident on Interstate 580. The one with the semi," he says to clarify.

I suck in my breath, trying to keep my composure as I feel the room spinning. My body feels frigid. Ethan's hand is now rubbing my back.

He leans over to whisper in my ear, "Breathe."

Exhaling slightly, I look down at my knotted hands in my lap, asking, barely audible, "Are they the two survivors airlifted, or were they part of the fatalities?" My eyes slowly come up to meet Officer Chavez's regard.

"I'm sorry. They did not make it, Miss Morgan. They were dead on arrival," he says with sympathy etched on his face.

My eyes close. I just sit there, praying that this is all a bad dream, that when I open my eyes, I will be lying back downstairs on the couch, wrapped in Ethan's arms, and we are being woken up by my very angry father threatening to kill Ethan for touching his little princess.

After a few moments, Officer Chavez speaks. "Miss Morgan. We will need you to come identify their bodies. Would you like to do that now or later today?"

The officer's voice brings me back to the nightmare that is now my reality. I stare blankly at him as my brain processes everything that I've just been told. I'm not sure how long it takes me to finally speak, but I state that I would like to go now.

"I'll drive you, Lexi," Ethan offers with another squeeze to my knotted hands.

"I can do this on my own. You don't have to drive me," I say to Ethan with no life in my voice.

"It's not up for discussion. You are not in the right state of mind to drive yourself," he retorts.

"I agree with your friend, Miss Morgan. For your safety and the safety of other drivers on the road, I suggest you let Ethan drive you."

Finally agreeing with both of them that I really should not be driving, I reply, "Please give me a couple of minutes to grab my purse and keys."

"Take your time, Miss Morgan. I will wait outside for you. Once you are ready, I will lead you to where your parents are," Officer Chavez says kindly.

It's probably close to six o'clock in the morning by the time Ethan gets me back home. I'm in a daze and have lost all sense of time since Officer Chavez showed up at my door. Everything is a complete blur. The only thing I can remember is arguing with Ethan to stay outside in the car while I went in to identify my parents' bodies. It was something I needed and insisted I do alone. I don't even remember coming back out to him, getting into the car, or driving back over the bay.

He pulls into his driveway. I open the car door to get out and close it softly behind me. Methodically I start to walk back over to my house, fishing my keys out of my purse.

Ethan comes up beside me and puts his hand on my lower back, sending a shock through me. That little gesture makes me realize that I am home and not sure how I even got here.

Shaking the unease away, I turn to him. "Thank you for driving me. I will be fine now."

"I'm not leaving you. You just found out your parents have died, and you had to identify their bodies. It's been a long night for both of us, and you really shouldn't be alone. Save your breath and don't argue. I'm coming inside with you," he commands.

"Whatever," I concede, with no energy to argue with him on this.

# Chapter Five

It's too hot, and that's what wakes me up. I'm still fully dressed, lying on top of the covers on my bed, with Ethan's body wrapped around me like he was before the officer showed up. I glance over to my night-stand and see that it's a little after three o'clock in the afternoon. I gently remove Ethan's arm from my waist so I can go to the bathroom. He stirs a little bit and rolls over the other way, hugging my other pillow, and I hear him make an "mmmmm" sound while inhaling deeply. He must like my scent to get that sound from him when he's asleep.

I swing my legs over the side of my bed and walk to my bathroom, closing the door behind me. Once I'm done doing my business, I brush my teeth and turn on my shower. I strip out of my clothes and step into the shower. As soon as the hot water hits my body, the reality of everything hits me like a freight train, and the tears start to fall, my body shuddering the harder I cry. I feel dizzy and weak, and my breaths are coming in short, frequent gasps, as I'm on the verge of hyperventilating. I can't stand anymore with my body convulsing, so I slide down the shower wall to sit on the floor with my back to the wall, knees pulled to my chest, and I rest my forehead on my knees as the rain showerhead runs the hot water over me.

I don't know how long I've been in the shower or how long I've been sitting there, but it was long enough that my hot water turned ice cold.

Being in a numb, dazed state, I didn't even notice. Just like I didn't notice Ethan coming into the bathroom until I hear, "What the fuck?" and feel his strong arms cradling me, lifting me from the floor.

"Your body is freezing and your lips are purple." His voice is laced with concern while removing me from the shower, sitting me on my vanity, and immediately wrapping my pink robe around me. He turns back around to shut off the shower, and it's then that I notice that he is still fully clothed and dripping wet.

"Lexi, look at me, baby," he pleads.

Now that I'm removed from the cold water, my body begins shaking uncontrollably. Slowly, I bring my eyes to meet his, and his brows are creased with worry.

"Are you OK to sit here for a minute?" he asks.

I just nod. My teeth are starting to chatter from being in the cold water, and I can't seem to find my voice at the moment. He rubs his hands up and down the sides of my robe, trying to warm me up a little bit, before he turns his back to me to face my bathtub and begins to remove his soaked clothing.

He takes off his shirt first, allowing me to admire the golden muscles in his back and traps as they flex when he rings the water out in the bathtub. He lays his shirt over the side of the tub and proceeds to remove his jeans and repeat the process. I'm not sure if he goes commando or if his underwear came down with his jeans, but I now have the spectacular view of his naked firm ass. I hear him clear his throat, and my eyes snap back up to meet his eyes staring back at me with heated desire.

"Towel, please," he says with a smirk.

Although I'm still freezing, I feel my face heat up as everything below my waist hums with a deep need. I snap my legs together in an effort to alleviate the aching as I shakily hand him the folded towel that is on the counter next to me. Once he grabs the towel, I immediately turn my head away from him.

"Hey, I'm decent now," he says with a hint of humor in his voice. "There's no need to be embarrassed."

I turn my head slowly to face him again. My attention immediately goes to the sexy V right above where the towel rests on his hips. I slowly rake in the vision of him as my eyes travel up his carved abs to his chiseled chest, before I finally stop at the hooded gray eyes that stare back at me with flashes of desire dancing through them. This man is built like an Adonis, and I want to do very naughty things with him.

I lick my lips as he comes over, placing his hands on my knees to spread my legs so he can step between them. His hands slide higher, stopping at my thighs, his thumbs lightly rubbing my inner thighs. "Are you warmer now?"

"I-I'm getting there," I stutter, but not from being cold. A robe and a towel are all that separate our naked bodies from touching flesh to flesh. I want more than anything to drop the towel that is around his waist so I can admire everything that makes Ethan a man built for sex. But my sadness and fear win the internal battle over my curiosity. I settle on thanking him for saving me from freezing to death.

"Thank you."

"That right there is exactly why I didn't want to leave you here alone, Lex."

"I know." My voice is laced with embarrassment.

Ethan brings his face within a breath of mine, and just as his lips graze mine, we hear my doorbell ring. We both startle at the sound, our heads turning in unison toward the direction of the bathroom door. He glances back at me before he takes a step back from between my legs, placing his hands on my waist for support as I slide off the vanity so I can go answer the door. I slide my arms into the sleeves of my robe and wrap it tight around my body before tying the belt.

"I'll be right back," I tell him in hope that he will stay in my room.

Before I can walk out of my bathroom, he pulls me back toward him and kisses my forehead and then the tip of my nose before placing another one of his featherlight kisses on my mouth.

"I will be right here if you need me," he offers in support.

The doorbell rings again before I can get to it. I finally open the door to see George and Marie Miller, Devin's parents. I'm surprised, and I just stand there frozen when Marie starts crying, grabs me in her arms, and embraces me tightly. It takes me a second to hug her back, and then my tears start to fall freely again. Being in her arms brings back the memory of what I just had to do earlier that morning.

"We came right over when we heard your parents' names listed as victims of the fatalities from the 580 accident," George offers in explanation.

"Oh, sweetheart, we are so sorry," Marie says between sobs.

My parents were best friends with Marie and George, so it shouldn't be a surprise that they are here. For all intents and purposes, George and Marie are like an uncle and aunt to me since I don't have any other family.

Marie finally releases her hold on me, and then George instantly grabs me into a big bear hug, kissing the top of my head. I can feel his body shake like he is trying to hold back his grief and be strong for his wife and me. I take a deep breath and inhale his scent. The cologne immediately reminds me of my dad, since they wore the same one. This is all too much too quick, so I push back off of him. "I-I-I can't do this right now." My voice falters, tears staining my cheeks.

I run up to my room, leaving George and Marie dumbfounded at the bottom of the stairs, and slam my doors shut. I'm leaning against them when Ethan rushes to my side and wraps me in his arms, holding me snug to his body. I wrap my arms around his waist, breathing in his scent, trying to erase my dad's. My lips lightly brush against his chest, and I hear Ethan let out a slight moan at the contact.

"Who's here?" he asks, concerned.

"George and Marie. They're my parents' best friends," I answer. I don't know why I omit that they are also Devin's parents. "It's too much right now. George smells like my dad, and I just couldn't take it."

"Do you want me to go downstairs and ask them to come back later?"

I look at him still wearing only a towel, and I place my forehead to his chest, shaking my head. "I will be OK. I just needed a moment to myself and to put some clothes on so I don't feel so vulnerable."

"Lex, you are vulnerable right now regardless of the clothing situation. You don't have to be the strong one. You have every right to be grieving."

"I'm going to change. Once I'm changed, I will go back downstairs and take them down to the family room or out back, so you can go home and get dry clothes," I tell Ethan.

"OK, but I will come back, Lexi," he says in a no-bullshit tone.

"I didn't think you wouldn't," I say over my shoulder as I head into my closet.

Ethan is sitting on my bed when I emerge from my closet wearing black yoga pants and an off-the-shoulder sweatshirt. I cross over to my bathroom, run my comb through my wet hair, and put it up in a messy wet bun on the top of my head before I head back downstairs.

"Are you just going to wear the towel home?" I question him.

"Yeah, it's only two houses over, Lex," he says as he stands up to walk over to where I am. He brings his left hand up to cup my right cheek and places another soft kiss on my lips. "I will see you later."

"OK."

I open my door and head back downstairs to find George and Marie in the kitchen. I walk to the refrigerator and grab a sugar-free

Red Bull.

"I'm sorry for how I acted when you hugged me, George," I apologize.

"Oh, honey, it's OK. We know this is a lot to handle. That's why we are here. We want to be here for you," Marie says. George gives me a warm smile.

"I need some air. Do you guys want to go sit out back?"

"Sure, honey," George agrees.

We head downstairs and out to the backyard. I glance back to the sliding glass door, knowing that Ethan will be sneaking out the front door any minute.

After we are outside sitting down on the lounge chairs and I know Ethan can't hear me, I ask in a low voice, "Where's Devin?"

Marie looks over at me with concern and sympathy. Before she answers, she glances at George and then turns back to tell me, "He's down in San Diego. The coaches made the whole team go down to support the cheer squad at regionals since the cheer squad is always cheering for them at the football games."

"It's good he wasn't here," I say after taking a drink from my Red Bull can.

It's quiet for a few moments before we all hear loud voices coming from the front of the house. I jump up and dart inside, up the stairs, and out the front door to find Ethan in just my towel with his wet clothes in hand and my ex–best friend face-to-face, hatred radiating off both of them.

"I'm going to ask one more time, what the fuck are you doing here, asshole?" Ethan's voice spews venom.

"Fuck off. I don't have to answer to you," Devin replies with equal vehemence.

I run down the front steps and step between these two livid men who look ready to throw down at any moment.

"What the hell is going on, you two?" I ask with a shaky voice.

"I was coming to check on you after I heard what happened, and when I pulled up, this douche bag was leaving your house in a fucking towel," Devin says, glancing down at me with hurt and anger in his eyes.

"Devin!" Marie yells.

His head snaps up to see both his mother and father standing on the porch. I'm standing there between two very big, very pissed off men, and I don't know what I could possibly do to prevent them from a physical fight if it came down to it.

"Run along, Devin. Mommy is calling you." Ethan seethes with sarcasm.

Devin's attention immediately shoots back to Ethan, eyes narrowed. "So, what, you come over here and pretend to comfort Lexi so you can fuck her?" he rages.

"Oh my God, Devin! What the fuck? Leave or go inside, now!" I scream at him.

"Ethan, go home. I will talk to you later," I snap.

He looks down at me, and without skipping a beat, he wraps his free arm around my waist, pulling me to him, and his mouth crushes to mine, staking his claim on me.

I push him off. I'm so pissed that I yell at him, "Go home!" Jesus. He might as well have lifted his leg and urinated on me to mark his territory.

"I will be back later, Lexi. Don't forget that." Ethan says the first part to me, but I have the distinct feeling the second part was meant for Devin.

I shake my head and turn to walk back to my house when I notice an older phantom black Audi A5 parked next to Devin's parents' Ford F-150. It has the S-Line package—blacked out windows and all-black powder-coated five-spoke wheels. He must have got a new car, and that's why I didn't hear him drive up in the very loud Chevelle.

Devin is following me back toward my house, and as soon as we are inside with the door shut, I turn around and slap him across the face with everything I have. The look on his face and his parents' was of disbelief. Neither of his parents move, nor do they say a word.

"What the hell, Lexi?" Devin says as he rubs his left cheek.

"'What the hell, Lexi' is all you have to say to me after total silence for the past two years?" I spit back at him.

"Alexa," Marie interrupts, "George and I are going to head home. It's obvious you and Devin have some things to talk about and work out. We want to come back tomorrow to help you with funeral arrangements and anything else you may need." She comes over to me and places her hands on my shoulders and a kiss on my cheek. "We love you, honey."

"We'll see you at home, Son," George says to Devin, patting him on the back.

"Yeah, Dad," Devin answers, but his eyes never leave my face.

"I love you both too, and I appreciate you both coming over to be with me. I will call you when I am ready to start dealing with funeral arrangements. Tomorrow will not be the day," I say. My voice starts to crack again.

"Just let us know what you need, OK, honey?" Marie reiterates.

"I will. Bye, George. Bye, Marie," I say as they walk out my front door.

◡৶

I walk downstairs to the bar, grab a shot glass, and poor myself a shot of Jack Daniel's. I guess that was what I was drinking last night before everything in my life was turned upside down. I shoot it quickly, remembering I like the burn I feel as it slides down my throat. I pour a second one and down it just as fast as the first one.

"So, what? You drink now?" Devin asks coldly.

"What makes you think I haven't been drinking these past two years?" I snap back.

"Look, Lexi, I flew back up from San Diego early so I could be here for you."

"No one asked you to do that, Devin." The tone of my voice is filled with pain and anger.

"Goddammit, Lex!" he chides as he steps up to me by the bar and grabs me in a tight hug. "Let me be here for you. Please?" he begs in a quiet voice.

As soon as I feel Devin's arms wrap around me, I lose the last bit of my strength and control. The dam breaks into a river of tears, and my gut-wrenching sobs are back in full force.

"Oh my God!" I scream as I drop to my knees on the floor, taking Devin with me. "Why is this happening to me? What did I do to deserve to be left without my parents?" My body convulses as more sobs rake through it.

"Sh, sh, sh, baby girl. You didn't do anything. It was an accident," Devin says, one arm wrapped around my back and the other holding the back of my head to his chest as he tries to soothe my shuddering body.

Pushing back, I shout, "Fuck the accident! This isn't supposed to be like this! This isn't my life. They should be here right now, not dead! My dad and I should be putting the motor in the Cobra while Mom sits and drinks her wine. I will never get to do that with him. I will never get that back." I lean my forehead on Devin's chest and continue crying.

"I'm here, and I won't leave you. I'm sorry you're going through this nightmare. I'm sorry I never called or texted you. I just didn't know, and I still don't know, how I can be friends with you when I'm in love with you, but I realize now that I don't ever want to be without you again."

"You hurt me, Dev," I say, sniffling. "You never gave us a chance to work it out after you left. I've been miserable these last two years without my best friend."

We sit in silence, holding on to each other on the floor in my family room as time ticks away. Devin finally shifts me away and stands up, holding his hand out to me so he can help me up. I willingly take it, and he pulls me back to my feet.

Devin's blue eyes are dark and a little bloodshot, like he was crying too, as he gazes down into my puffy, red-rimmed eyes. He asks me, "Are you hungry?"

I shake my head. I'm just now really seeing Devin for the first time since his heated argument with Ethan. He's taller since I last saw him, with broader shoulders, large biceps, and big strong hands that are slightly calloused, and I can see his well-defined torso beneath his fitted T-shirt.

I shake off the strange feeling that is fluttering around in my stomach as I turn back toward the bar to pour another shot of Jack. I just want to be numb right now, lost in a hazy fog that only Jack Daniel's can provide.

"You really shouldn't drink that on an empty stomach," Devin says, concerned.

"You don't get a say in what I do, Devin. You're the one who tossed our friendship out the window. If you want to stay here, then stay, but I don't need you lecturing me on what I should or should not do right now." I sneer at him.

"You're right. I don't. Well, pour me one too, then."

I submit to his request, grab a second shot glass, and pour him a shot of whiskey. I always heard my dad say that it's never good to drink alone. We both shoot back the whiskey, and Devin coughs as it goes down.

"Oh God, that is harsh shit," he says with a disgusted look on his face.

Seeing his nose scrunch up and eyes water a little bit makes me laugh.

"You always were a wimp, Dev," I say jokingly.

"Screw you. Pour me another. I need to catch up," he orders. I pour him another shot. This time, I hear him hold his breath before he pounds back the shot.

"Ugh! How in the hell do you drink this crap?"

"Never had a sip until yesterday," I confess.

"Well, you're downing it like a pro."

I smile up at him, and then I wrap my arms back around his waist and lay my head against his chest over his heart. I can hear and feel the pace of his heartbeat speed up by this simple gesture. He brings his arms around my shoulders and holds me there, placing a light kiss to the top of my head before resting his cheek there. Right now, I don't care how much hurt I've experienced over the last couple of years because of his absence; it feels right to have Devin with me when I need him the most, when I need him to be my rock and help me get through the loss of my parents whom he knew very well and cared about too.

"Congratulations on Stanford and happy eighteenth birthday, Lexi." His voice breaks into the comfortable silence that has been surrounding us for the past few minutes.

I inhale a deep, stuttering breath as tears start to burn my eyes again. My emotions are raw and all over the place. I will never get to tell my parents about Stanford. They will never know their little girl got into her school of choice. They won't get to see me graduate high school or college or see me get married someday. My dad will never see his car complete.

"Thank you, Devin. You were the first person I told. Only one other person knows I got my early acceptance letter."

"Ethan?" he questions as his body goes rigid.

"Yes. He has been here since the earthquake hit yesterday."

"Are you with him, Lex?"

"No, I'm not."

"Are you sleeping with him?"

"That is none of your business, Dev." My voice is laced with irritation as I release my hug.

"Just tell me, Lexi. I need to know if he has you."

"No, dammit! He doesn't have me and hasn't had me. Are you satisfied now?" My temper is boiling over right now. My parents just died, and he's questioning me about my neighbor.

"Why was he leaving here in just a towel, then, if you're not fucking him?"

"Jesus Christ, Devin! Do you have no filter or boundaries right now? My parents just died. Did you come here to comfort me or question me about my fucking love life?"

"I'm sorry. I saw him in a towel and saw red the second he kissed you. I really am here to be your friend and to comfort you. It's just hard fighting my feelings for you, and my mind is confused at the moment."

"Well, you are making it very hard to believe that you are here as my friend, and I'm sorry it's hard for you. Again, I didn't ask you to be here, Devin," I say, turning to pour another shot.

"I know you didn't, and I am sorry," he apologizes again while looking at the shot I just poured.

I hold the bottle up, asking the silent question if he wants another shot. He nods, so I pour him another as well. Another shot slides down smoother than the last, and I'm starting to feel the effects when my phone chimes with a text message.

Jessa: OMG Lex! We just heard!!!! We are on our way!

Me: No. I'm ok at the moment. Dev is here. Thanks for checking on me. I will text you guys later.

Jessa: He is? R u sure u don't want us to come over?

Me: It's fine right now.

Jessa: Ok girl. We r here 4 u. ANY TIME!

Me: I know u r. Thx. XO

Jessa: XO

"The twins," I offer before he could ask.

"I didn't say anything."

"You didn't have to. The look on your face was enough."

"Am I that transparent?"

"Yes."

There is a knock at my front door, and I already know who it is before I even answer it. Devin's eyes narrow in anger, as I'm sure he knows too. It's been about an hour and half since Ethan left my house. I'm actually surprised he stayed away this long, knowing Devin is here. I thought for sure he would have come right back when he saw George and Marie leave.

"I don't want any fighting, do you understand?" I say in a stern tone.

"I will do my best," he replies, noncommittal.

I turn to go up the stairs and stumble a little before I get to them. I must be buzzed because I need the handrail to get up the stairs to answer the front door. There's a bang on the door before I reach it.

"Hold on, dammit! I'm coming." My words are slightly slurred. OK, maybe I'm a lot buzzed when I don't even recognize my own voice.

I make it to the door and unlock it to see Ethan staring down at me, his brows furrowed in anger at the sight he sees. I sway a little, opening the door wider so he can come inside.

"What the fuck happened to you?" Ethan asks, concerned.

"Whah? Me? Nothing. Oh, wait, my parents died. That's what happened to me," I answer with narrowed eyes, poking his chest. I'm beginning to really feel the shots I took.

"You're fucking drunk!" he shouts.

"And your point, Mr. Gage?" I say with sarcasm.

"Have you at least eaten?"

"No, she hasn't," Devin interrupts from the stairs.

"Nice one, asshole. You let her get fucked up when she's grieving," Ethan fumes.

"Fuck you! I tried to stop her, and I tried to get her to eat," Devin retorts.

"Hey! Stop it, both of you," I yell as I sway a little more.

They stop arguing as they watch me carefully. I shake my head in an effort to clear some of the alcohol-induced haze, but that small movement makes me stumble sideways. Both men hurry to catch me before I fall over. I'm sandwiched between the two hard pillars that are Ethan and Devin. The feel of both of their hands on my body sends a ripple of pleasure through me. Both remove their hands and take a step back once they see my balance has returned. My body shivers from the loss of their touch, and a ghost of a laugh escapes my lips as I look between the two men. Thoughts that shouldn't be fluttering around in my mind are up front and present. I wonder what it would be like to have my body worshiped by these two gorgeous guys at the same time. "It would be truly amazing," I whisper out loud.

"What's that?" Ethan asks.

"What?" I say in confusion as I look at Ethan.

"You just said something, Lexi. What was it?" Devin asks the question this time.

"Shit, nothing. Just thinking out loud, apparently," I answer, flustered, blood rising to my cheeks. Once I have my bearings somewhat straight, I turn to Ethan again. "Um, Ethan, I appreciate you being here last night through everything, but I need some time alone with Devin. He was very close to my parents too, and I need to fix this because I need him in my life right now. Please don't be upset. I need you to understand. I will see you tomorrow, OK?" I ask.

"I don't like you drinking without eating, Lexi. I will leave and give you your time if you promise me you will eat something now, not later," he negotiates.

"Fine, Mr. Bossy. I will make a sandwich right now, and I will drink some water. I promise." I give him a half-assed Scout's honor and sway a little, trying to keep my focus on him. Devin went back downstairs at some point during this conversation.

"Come here," Ethan says and pulls me into his arms. He smells like heaven. His musky bodywash mixed with his laundry detergent makes me want to stay in this embrace forever. "I'll see you first thing in the morning, Lexi. And just for the record, I don't like this at all," he declares.

"I'll see you tomorrow, Ethan," I say, kissing his cheek.

He kisses my temple and turns to walk out the door, closing it behind him as he leaves. I lock it and lean against it for some support. My head is definitely dazed. I cross the foyer over to the kitchen so I can make myself a sandwich and drink some water.

"Do you want a sandwich, Dev?"

"Sure," he says, coming up the stairs to the kitchen holding two more shots. I know he purposefully brought more alcohol up in defiance of Ethan.

Last time we were in this kitchen together, he kissed me and walked out of my life for two years. I suddenly feel uneasy.

"Here." He offers the shot to me.

"Thanks."

"Cheers," he says as we clank our shot glasses together, and we each do our shots.

"Well, I'm feeling pretty damn good right now," Devin says with a slight sway of his own before he leans his hip to the center island for support.

"Here. Drink this." I offer him a bottle of water. He takes it and chugs it like he's been in the desert without water for days.

"Thank you. I needed that."

I finish making our pepper turkey on sliced sourdough sandwiches, and we take our seats at the dining table, eating in silence and drinking waters, trying to rehydrate.

"Hey. I texted my mom and told her I was staying here tonight. Plus, I don't think I should drive home in my condition."

"I don't think you should either. It really is nice having you here right now," I say honestly.

"You don't have to put on a strong front, Lex. I'm here to comfort you. If you need or want to cry or scream at the tops of your lungs, please don't hold back."

"I know. I'm not sure how I feel or what I want at this moment. I think the alcohol has temporarily hindered me."

Devin grabs a couple of beers from the refrigerator, and we head out to the backyard. We go to the hot tub, and Devin kicks off his Chucks. We both sit on the edge with our feet in the warm water. Even though I disliked beer when my dad gave me a sip, this one isn't so bad. It could be because I don't have taste buds anymore from the shots.

We sit and talk about everything and nothing. He tells me that he's maintained his 4.0 GPA taking college prep classes and is still the varsity quarterback and senior class president.

"Very impressive, Devin. What about a girlfriend?"

"I've dated a couple of girls, but neither felt right."

I'm not sure why, but I actually don't like the fact that he has dated. The fact that another girl got to enjoy his kisses and his hugs really bothers me. At this point, I don't want to know if they got to enjoy any other part of him.

"Oh," is all I can get out.

Devin gets up, goes over to my pool house, and grabs us each another beer from the refrigerator. After he sets them down, he takes off his shirt. His muscles flex as he pulls the thin material over his head and drops the shirt to the ground. He then unbuttons his jeans and pulls them off, leaving him in just his boxer briefs. His perfectly ripped abs cut down to the sexy V just above his waistband, and a hint of his happy trail vanishes below the waistband.

Feeling my face get hot, I turn away so he can't see the crimson blush. I ask, "What are you doing?"

"Getting in the water. What does it look like?" He slides into the hot tub.

"Oh. OK."

"Join me."

"Let me go change."

"No. If you have a bra and underwear on, you don't need to change."

"But, Dev—"

"Don't be a wuss," he teases, cutting me off before I can finish my sentence.

"Fine," I say nervously. I pull my sweatshirt over my head and drop it to the ground. I'm standing in my hot-pink push-up lace bra that enhances my cleavage just enough and yoga pants. I slowly hook my thumbs into the waist of my yoga pants, slide them over my firm backside and down my toned legs, and step out of them. I keep my body tight and in shape by doing gymnastics and cheer. No matter what I do, though, I still have curvy hips. My dad says that trait is from my biological mother. The only mom I knew was Jeanine, and now she and my dad are both gone. God, this sucks.

"My God, you are fucking beautiful," Devin says in admiration after I have shucked my clothes.

Devin's words shake me from my thoughts. "Um, thanks," I say as I slide down into the water with just my bra and matching cheeky panties on.

"Here," Devin says, handing me another beer.

We clink our bottles together and both take a drink. The cold beer is refreshing since we're sitting in a very warm hot tub. As the sun begins to set and the October sky is brilliant shades of orange, we continue our comfortable conversation and enjoy being reunited even if it's because of a tragic circumstance.

# Chapter Six

O uch. My head is throbbing. If this is what a hangover feels like, I don't like it. I glance at my alarm clock and see that it's only three twenty in the morning. I roll over onto my back, and just as I do, an arm swings over my middle and lips graze my bare shoulder. I freeze instantly, trying to remember what happened after the hot tub. It's all a blur. I am thankful that I'm still wearing my bra and panties, but that doesn't mean anything. Oh God! Did I kiss Devin again? Did we do more than kiss? My mind is racing, trying to remember.

I slide out from under Devin's arm and cross over to my bathroom, quietly closing the door before turning on the light. Once I'm in there, I splash cold water on my face. I don't even recognize the reflection staring back at me. I have no color in my cheeks, and my eyes are swollen with dark circles under them. I look like death. I quickly brush my teeth, then grab a bottle of ibuprofen, dump four into my hand, and toss them to the back of my throat while I grab a cup on my counter and fill it with water to chase the pills.

"Come on, Lex, think," I whisper to myself, hoping I can remember a shred of what went on with Devin last night. I startle when there's a light knock on the bathroom door.

"Are you OK?" Devin's groggy voice whispers through the door.

"I'm fine. I needed some ibuprofen."

"Would you leave some out for me too? My head feels like it was hit with a baseball bat."

I lean over toward the door and open it. Devin's eyes squint from the brightness, and he rubs his face with both hands. He's only wearing his boxer briefs, and I can't help but take in the stunning sight before me. My God, he is breathtaking just standing there in my bathroom doorway, half asleep and very much hungover.

"Fuck me. The pounding in my head is killing me," he grumbles as he rubs his temples.

"I'm right there with ya. Here." I pour four ibuprofens into his hand and give him my cup with water in it.

"Thanks."

"I'll let you use the restroom in peace. I'm going to lie back down."

"OK."

I close the door to the bathroom and head downstairs to grab a couple bottles of water. When I come back to the room, Devin is just coming out of the bathroom, looking a little more refreshed.

"Here's some more water," I say as I hand him a bottle.

"Thanks. I used your toothbrush. I hope that's OK."

"Well, it's a little late now to question if it's OK," I say teasingly. "And yes, that's fine. I don't have cooties, and I trust you don't either."

"Yeah, I guess it is a little too late. I had cotton mouth, and it was not pleasant."

"Well, we can't have that now, can we?"

We both go back to my bed and crawl in.

I'm on my back staring up at the ceiling for a few minutes before I find the nerve to ask Devin what happened. I've been arguing with myself mentally if I really want to know the answer.

"Dev, what happened last night?"

"What do you mean what happened? Nothing happened. We were in the hot tub getting shitfaced, and then you started crying, so I told you we should go back inside. Once we were out of the hot tub and back in the house, your crying turned to hysterics when you went into your parents' bedroom. It was crazy and a little scary that you went from crying to laughing. After a while of sitting in your dad's closet, I carried you up to your room, tucked you into bed, and told you I was going to sleep in the spare bedroom across the hall, but you begged me to hold you until you fell asleep. It looks like I fell asleep too."

"The crying and hysterics explains why I look like death. Thank you for staying with me and not taking advantage of a hysterical drunk girl. I know it couldn't have been easy for you."

"First of all, you still look beautiful, even if you're a hot mess. Second, I would never take advantage of you or any other girl when they are hammered. Third, I will always be here for you. I'm not going anywhere ever again. I'm sorry I wasn't around the past two years."

"Dev, will you hold me again until we both fall back to sleep?"

"Of course. Come here." His arms open to invite me in.

I scoot my back to Devin's front, and he wraps his left arm around me, tucking me closer and tighter into his hard body. Where his head is lying, I can feel his hot breaths on my neck. It's sending ripples of chills down my spine, and I feel the goose bumps rising. I also feel the strange tug and tingle in my core. I start to imagine Devin's hand moving farther south to help relieve the ache that's throbbing between my thighs.

"Good night, Lex," he says as he brushes a kiss to my shoulder.

"Good night, Devin."

⌒᠀

I wake up with Devin's hand resting on my thigh, and I can feel his morning hard-on pressing against my backside.

"Dev, time to wake up," I whisper, so as not to startle him.

He mumbles something, and the hand that was on my thigh slides up my side and cups my left breast. I feel his hips flex, pressing his morning wood harder against my butt. I suck in my breath and don't move. As scared as I am to move right now, his simple movement made my stomach do a flip, and the heat between my legs has ignited again. I don't want to ruin my friendship with him, but this feels so good being in his arms in my bed.

I can't help that my mind wanders to the land of sultry sex, and I wonder what it would be like to lose my virginity to Devin. I have no doubt that with him it would be slow lovemaking. We would take our time, exploring each other's bodies, learning each other's erogenous zones. It would be intimately sweet.

With Ethan, I visualize down and dirty fucking. No sweetness about it. He would demand or just take what he wanted from my body. All control would be his. With him, I would be a sweaty, sexed-up mess. Either option has my sex clenched tight and my clit throbbing, begging for attention.

My mom explained to me about masturbation and sex toys when I turned seventeen, but I always felt weird about touching myself so I never tried it. She even gave me a couple of pornos to watch so I could have a better understanding of all things sex without all the clinical jargon that sex education tapes are littered with. They definitely were informative and hot. Mom further explained that sex and masturbation are not something to be ashamed of and to enjoy the feelings of pleasure that I would get from either act. One would think that was an awkward conversation to have with a parent, but my mom and I were very close. There wasn't anything I couldn't talk to her about.

Right now, in this moment, I honestly think I could get past the masturbation weirdness if Devin wasn't in my bed holding on to me. Some relief from all this sexual tension would be very welcome. I feel like I'm wound tight and ready to snap into a million pieces.

I hear a faint knock on the front door, and the noise pulls me from my very inappropriate thoughts of my best friend and my neighbor. I glance at my alarm clock, and it's a little after eight in the morning now. Ethan, oh, fuck. I jump up out of bed and run into my closet to put clothes on. There is no way he would believe nothing happened, since the last time he saw me I was drunk and made him leave me alone with Devin.

"What's wrong?" Devin asks sleepily.

"Nothing. Ethan is here. He said he would be back this morning."

"Fucking fantastic," he snaps, flopping back onto the pillow and throwing an arm over his eyes.

"Dev, please be civil this morning for me."

"Whatever. Better not keep Mr. Wonderful waiting," he says with a wave of his hand, as if he is shooing me away.

It's amazing how just moments ago I was imagining making love to Devin, and now I want to kick his ass. Men are so frustrating.

I leave my room, closing the doors after I walk out, and head down to the front door.

As soon as I open the door, I'm taken aback at Ethan's appearance. He looks disheveled, like he's hungover and hasn't slept.

"Hey," I say sweetly with a small smile on my face.

"God, you're beautiful in the morning," he says, stepping inside and capturing me in his arms. He breathes me in with his nose nestled in the crook of my neck, and a slight moan escapes his lips. "I missed you last night."

He definitely tied one on last night, because I can smell the alcohol seeping from his pores mixed with his bodywash.

"Oh, really? You look like you were out partying all night."

"I was pissed leaving you here drunk and alone with someone who is in love with you. I went home and polished off a fifth of Jack and some beers. I couldn't sleep because I kept thinking he was the one who would get to fuck you last night."

The last words shock me. I don't know whether to be pissed that he thought so little of me or flattered that he was jealous of Devin. Again, men are so frustrating.

I choose to brush it off since he looks like shit and probably doesn't realize what he just said. "Let me make you some coffee," I offer as I pull from his embrace and head to the kitchen.

"Where is lover boy?"

"Upstairs sleeping."

"Where did he sleep, Lexi?"

I glance over my shoulder, giving him a dirty look as I answer, "Not that it's any of your business, Ethan, but he slept in my bed with me."

His face turns to stone, and his gray eyes turn cold as a storm brews in them. They look intently into mine as he crosses the short distance between us.

"Did you fuck him?"

"Whah?" I gape with my mouth open. "Holy hell! You both need to have your heads examined."

"I'm only going to ask you this once, Lexi, and you better not lie to me. Did he touch you in any way?"

"Ethan, you are being jealous and stupid."

"Lex, you are trying my patience," he warns.

"Yes, he touched me. He held me as we slept together. I asked. No, wait, I begged him to stay and hold me since I was a blubbering, drunk mess because my parents just died! Do you feel better now that you know?"

"Lex, are you OK?" Devin asks as he comes into the kitchen with bare feet, one button on his jeans still undone, showing just a hint of his happy trail, pulling his shirt over his head.

"I'm fine," I snap unintentionally, since it's Ethan who I'm mad at.

"You can leave now, Devin. I will take care of my girl from here."

"Fuck off. I will leave when I'm ready."

"Both of you need to stop this childish behavior. I can't take it right now," I squeak out as my voice cracks, and a lonely tear streaks down my cheek.

"I'm sorry, Lex," Devin says apologetically as he walks over to hug me, placing a kiss on the crown of my head, all while glaring at Ethan. "I'm going to head home, but I will be back later with my parents, OK?"

"That's fine. Thank you again for being here with me last night. It meant a lot to me."

Devin turns, pushing past Ethan, and I follow so I can walk him out to his car. He bends to grab his shoes, which he left by the door before coming into the kitchen, and we head outside. Once we are standing by his car, I ask, "Hey, where's the Chevelle?"

He smiles at me, and it makes my heart flutter again before he answers, "I still have it. She's in the garage at home. I needed a car that still had speed but gets better gas mileage when I start commuting to Stanford."

"What! You got into Stanford too, and you're just now telling me!" I scream excitedly.

"Yeah. It's on a football scholarship, but I got in."

"That is amazing, Devin. I'm so happy and proud of you." I jump up and wrap my arms around his neck, smacking a kiss to his cheek.

"It is pretty amazing. Anyway, douche bag is waiting for you. I guess I will head home so I can shower and change. Do you want me to bring clothes back so I can crash here again with you?"

"Dev, you have school. I don't want you to miss school or jeopardize your scholarship because of me."

"Text me if you want me to stay. I'll see ya later."

"See ya."

I walk back into the house to find Ethan staring out the picture window in front of the sink with a cup of coffee in his hand.

"Now that you have had a cup of coffee, are you ready to be civil or will I still be dealing with the childish and jealous boy next door?" I ask coldly.

Looking down into the sink, he quietly answers, "I'm sorry for how I acted. I've never acted that way with any of the other women I've dated."

"We're not dating, Ethan. I'm not sure what this is. All I know is we are two people who have kissed a couple of times and slept in the same bed once."

Ethan turns to face me so I can see the sincerity in his tired gray eyes. "I want you to be mine and mine alone, Lexi. I've waited too long for you, and I don't plan to wait any longer."

Ethan's declaration has my mind spinning. I've wanted him, even fantasized and dreamed about having him, and here he is, standing in front of me telling me he wants me to be his. I should be ecstatic that the man of my dreams for all these years wants me, but frankly, the thought scares the hell out of me. I have never dated nor had a boyfriend. With my parents' untimely death, I can only imagine the shit storm that awaits when I start dealing with my loss, their lawyers, my home, Mom's business, and not to mention trying to get through the rest of my senior year so I can graduate and start my college education at Stanford.

"Ethan, I—"

Quickly coming over to where I'm standing, Ethan stops me before I have a chance to reply. "Sh. Just hear me out. I know you have a lot on your plate right now, and it's only going to get harder. I also understand it's not fair of me to put this on you, but my patience is at its limit waiting for you. Let me take you to breakfast so my words can sink in before you say anything."

I look up into his eyes, which are full of hope, and nod. "I will go to breakfast with you. Let me shower and get ready."

"OK. I will go home and do the same. I will meet you outside in an hour?"

"That will work."

⤳

We are sitting at an Irish pub in Millbrae for breakfast. Ethan greets our waitress by name. It's Mindy or Mandy or Muffy. Oh, who cares? He shoots her one of his panty-dropping smiles when he orders both of us a Bloody Mary, extra spicy. He says it's the "hair of the dog" or something to that effect. I'm shocked that I wasn't carded, since I know I don't look twenty-one, but maybe that's why he graced the waitress with one of his megawatt smiles.

The waitress brings us our drinks and winks at Ethan as she sashays away. I roll my eyes at the show she's trying to put on for him while blatantly disregarding my presence. I'm going to assume he gets this reaction a lot from women since I'm only getting to witness it firsthand for the first time.

"Cheers," he says as he clanks his glass to mine before taking a drink.

"Cheers," I say back before taking a sip. It's actually not bad, and you really don't taste the alcohol at all. I take a bigger drink and immediately start coughing. My eyes instantly water as I get a big gulp of the spiciness hitting the back of my throat. I'm guessing it's pepper mixed with Tabasco sauce, of which I'm generally not a fan.

"You OK there?" Ethan asks as he laughs boyishly.

"Uh-huh. Spicy," I choke out in an effort to explain after taking a sip of water.

"Ha! You should have seen the look on your face. It was priceless," he teases me.

"I'm glad I can amuse you," I grumble back at him.

"Oh, don't get upset. You have to admit it was funny."

"Whatever." My bottom lip juts out as I pout.

The rest of breakfast goes more smoothly. This restaurant doesn't mess around on their portions. My eyes nearly pop out of their sockets when I get my plate of scrambled eggs, bacon, and country fried potatoes. There's enough food to feed half of the cheer squad and myself.

This time, instead of ordering a Bloody Mary for me, Ethan orders me a vodka Red Bull. Now this is my kind of drink. Not only does it taste fantastic, it goes down a lot easier.

By the time we finish with breakfast, my plate looks like I barely touched it, but I am most definitely stuffed. Not to mention the fact that I had two vodka Red Bulls in pint glasses.

The waitress brings our check to the table and brushes her hand over Ethan's shoulder when she walks away. This girl has some balls on her. He laughs when he opens the leather check holder. I glance over and see that she wrote her phone number down and scrawled across the top, "Don't lose it this time!" I just shake my head.

"What?" he asks innocently as I again amuse him.

"Do women throw themselves at you often when you are out with another woman?"

He laughs a wholehearted, deep, bellowing laugh as he shakes his head. "She is relentless, Lex. I've never given her nor would I ever give her the time of day."

When he is done paying the check, we both stand to leave, and I get a little dizzy and immediately have to grab the back of my chair to keep from falling on my face.

"Wow. I just got a little dizzy standing up."

"Vodka Red Bulls will sneak up on ya. Are you good to walk to the car, or shall I put you over my shoulder and carry you out?"

"I'm perfectly capable of walking on my own, thank you."

Thankfully, I make it to his car without incident. We drive back to my house with the radio on. It takes me a second to realize he's listening to the Tiesto song that I had playing the other day when he scared me half to death. Then I notice that the music is streaming from his iPod. I glance over at Ethan with one eyebrow arched and catch his cocky smirk.

"It's my new favorite song," he offers without me asking.

A small smile tugs at my lips.

When Ethan pulls into his driveway, I can't believe it's only ten o'clock and I'm already buzzed. I will admit the drinks did help with the hangover, though. I will have to remember those in the future when I need "hair of the dog."

We walk over to my house, and once we are at my front door, I unlock it and hear my cell phone ringing from upstairs.

"Crap! I left my phone here," I mutter as I run up the stairs to my bedroom.

I grab my phone off of my nightstand and see that I have two missed calls from Marie Miller and three text messages from different people.

I immediately dial Marie back, putting her on speakerphone.

"Is everything OK, Lexi?" Marie asks, concerned.

"Yeah, sorry about that. I forgot my phone at home when I went to breakfast."

"It's OK, honey. I was just worried since I hadn't heard from you yet and Devin has been home for a while now."

"I'm OK. Really," I explain. "I'm just really not in the mind-set to do funeral arrangements today. Can we please do this tomorrow?"

"Of course, but we need to do it, Lexi," she scolds.

"I know what needs to be done, Marie, and I really appreciate you and George helping me. I just need one more day to get my head straight. That's all I'm asking for. This isn't easy for me."

"OK, Lexi. We will be over at five o'clock tomorrow after George gets home from work and you're home from school."

"That's fine. Thank you, Marie." I hit end.

Ethan is sitting on my bed, quietly waiting for me to acknowledge him.

I check my text messages and reply back to Devin first.

Me: Hey. Are you coming back today or tomorrow w/ ur parents?
Devin: Tomorrow. I figured I can grab my assignments and stay w/ u a cpl days.
Me: That sounds great. C u tomorrow.

Next, I do a group text to Jessa and Becca so I can kill two birds, or twins, with one stone.

Me: Hey. I'm doing ok. Just trying 2 sort thru feelings. I will see you both at school tomorrow. Pinky swear.
Becca: Ok skank. Luv ya!
Me: Luv ya bitch!
Jessa: Seriously, call if u need us. <3 u slut!
Me: I will. <3 ya whore

"So do I get you all to myself for the rest of the day, or do I have to share you with others?"

"It's just you and me today, but I can't guarantee that I won't have meltdowns throughout the day. I seem to be OK, and then one little thing or thought sends me into a tailspin."

"I'm here to comfort you and help you get through this," he says as he grabs me by the waist and pulls me between his legs where he's sitting on my bed.

My hands splay on his taut shoulders. I look down into his luminous eyes and lean my head down to lightly brush my lips back and forth over Ethan's lovely mouth. I lick his bottom lip, and he exhales a breath I didn't even realize he was holding. His mouth gradually opens, allowing my tongue to lick his tongue, tease his tongue, as his hands move from my waist and wrap around to my backside so he can grip my ass and pull me closer. A faint moan escapes my mouth as Ethan pulls back from our kiss, leaving me wanting more. He gently pushes me back away from him so he can stand. His powerful body now towers over my petite frame as he cups my face in his hands and kisses me breathless before he pulls back again. A small whimper exhales from my lips again in protest, and the slightest smile curves at the corner of his mouth.

"Do you want another drink?"

If this day is going to go how I think it is, I'm going to need another drink or two. "Sure. That actually sounds good."

He takes my hand, and we head downstairs to the bar in my family room. He grabs a couple of shot glasses and begins looking for the Jack. His eyes dart to mine with a hint of anger in them before he asks me, "Did you finish that bottle of Jack yesterday?"

"Well, I had some help," I counter.

"Right. I'm sure Devin was more than willing to help you get drunk."

"Don't start. If you are going to ruin a perfectly good morning by being a prick, then please leave and let me get on with my grieving alone."

His expression softens as he continues to move bottles of liquor around behind the bar. Then he smiles. "Well, this will do." He holds up a bottle of Macallan eighteen-year-old scotch. After unscrewing the cap, he switches the shot glasses for tumblers. He sees the confused look on my face and says, "This is expensive scotch. It's meant to be enjoyed slowly and not as a shot." I nod as I understand his explanation.

"In memory of your parents," he says as he holds up his tumbler.

I don't know what to say to that, so I just clink my tumbler to his and take a small sip. Now that was smooth. I take a bigger sip the second time, and it tastes better than the first.

"You might want to slow down just a tad. It is still early," he says with one eyebrow arched.

"And as I said before, you can leave if you are going to be a prick or start telling me what to do."

Ethan rounds the bar, grabs me by the waist, and pulls me to him, his mouth closing over mine. The feel of his tongue massaging mine is desperate, as if he will never get the opportunity to kiss me again. I lock my hands behind his neck, and he swiftly moves his strong, capable hands to my ass, lifting me as if I weighed as much as a kitten. I instinctively wrap my legs around his waist, locking my feet together at the ankles. At this angle, I can deepen the kiss a little more. He quickly turns toward the couch and lays me down. His body easily covers mine, emanating heated desire and a craving for only me. Ethan rocks his hips between my thighs and over my sensitive sex, drawing a moan out of me. His hardened length strains against his jeans, begging to be released. He begins to descend a trail of small nibbles and soft kisses from my mouth down my jawline to my neck. All the while, his right hand is deftly massaging and caressing my left breast.

"Ethan, please take me upstairs," I whisper. It almost sounds like begging. I feel a smile form on his lips at the base of my neck where his warm mouth is suckling. He places one last kiss at the hollow of my neck and quickly pushes off the couch, holding out his hand to help me up. I place my hand in his, and he pulls me to my feet and turns to head up the stairs to my bedroom.

As soon as we reach my room, Ethan turns to face me, grabbing the hem of my tank top and pulling it up over my head, leaving me in my lace camisole. Since the pink camisole is see-through, I know he is getting an eyeful of my heavy-with-need breasts and taut nipples, erect and awaiting his touch. A carnal growl escapes him.

"Those are the most luscious and perfect pair of breasts I have ever seen. Women cannot buy your tits, baby."

I feel the heat rise straight to my cheeks and wetness pool between my thighs. I clamp them close together in an effort to alleviate the tingly sensation that is my throbbing clit. Despite the fact that Ethan has seen me completely nude, it was when I was in shock sitting on my shower floor. He picked me up and immediately covered me up after he removed me from the freezing cold water. I'm not even naked yet, and his eyes are intensely dark, devouring the sight before him.

I unbutton my jean shorts and drag the zipper down. I hook my index fingers into the side belt loops and slowly shimmy out of them, stepping one foot out and kicking the shorts away with the other. I'm wearing a lacy thong that matches the camisole perfectly. Mom always told me that my undergarments should always match and that women should always be neatly maintained in the southern region, which is why she and I went religiously to our esthetician for waxing. My God, I'm going to miss my mom. There is so much more I need to learn from both of my parents, and I will never get that chance.

I try to shake away the sadness that has suddenly crept up on me, hoping Ethan doesn't see the change. I have plenty of time to mourn my parents starting tomorrow. Today, I need this for me. I need to continue to feel, for I fear that if I go numb, I will not recover.

"You are absolutely stunning, Lexi. I will never get tired of staring into your mesmerizing eyes or looking at your beautiful face or touching this amazing body."

I say nothing as I step closer to Ethan, licking my lips. His words are intoxicating, and the way his lust-filled eyes rake over my body has fueled my courage to continue and set my libido ablaze. I reach for his shirt and pull it over his head. My body reacts with an electric shock straight to my sex just from the sight of his sculptured torso. I place a sensual kiss to his chest right where his heart beats, tenderly dragging the tip of my tongue over the flat disc of his nipple as my fingers work to undo his jeans, and continue a line of kisses down his abs as I pull his jeans down his powerful legs. His body tenses, and I hear him exhale a breath when I stand back up, meeting his hooded gaze.

"Talk to me, baby. You haven't said two words since we came up to your room." His voice is laced with worry.

"What is there to talk about when our body language seems to be doing just fine?" I ask with a shy glance up into his eyes.

"I just want to be sure we are both on the same page. That's all."

"Would I undress you, or allow you to undress me for that matter, if I wasn't on the same page?"

"Touché, Miss Morgan." A full smile is plastered on his face.

Ethan slides his hands under my camisole, gently sliding them up my abs and bringing the cami up over my breasts, stopping there as he takes my left nipple into his mouth and suckles it, licking it, teasing it. He then moves to the right nipple and repeats the same process. My head leans back, and my hands grab onto his hair as the assault continues on my breasts. A slight moan falls from my lips as Ethan's name follows on a whisper. He continues to remove the camisole completely, dropping it to the ground with our collection of discarded clothing.

I bring his mouth to mine, lick his lips, and draw his bottom lip into my mouth as I finally find the nerve to reach down and stroke his cock through his boxer briefs. Ethan bites down on my bottom lip hard, leaving the faint taste of copper that I'm guessing is because he drew blood when my hand found his hardened length.

"Lexi, you are going to completely unravel me," he says between his heavy breaths.

Taking a couple of steps away from him and toward my bed, I grab the sides of my thong and pull it down, leaving me completely and utterly vulnerable to Ethan Gage. The dark storm in his eyes blazes with a heated passion that I've never seen before this moment. I catch a glimpse of his fingers twitching, as if they yearn to touch me.

"Jesus Christ, woman. You are perfection."

A smile creeps across my lips as I climb onto my bed and lie back against the mountain of pillows. They keep me slightly propped up so my eyes never have to leave Ethan's.

He bends down quickly, grabbing something from his clothes on the floor, and then comes over to the left side of my bed. It's then that I see he put a couple of gold packets on my nightstand. I'm glad one of us is prepared. Then again, this is Ethan, player at heart, and me, the virtuous virgin. Of course he would be the prepared one.

With no hesitation, he drops his boxer briefs and grips his shaft, stroking his steel erection a few times before joining me on the bed. His pubic area is clean-shaven with only a dust of hair above his shaft. I don't know what I truly expected to see, but the length and girth of his perfect cock now has me terrified. All I can do is inhale a sharp breath as I drag my bottom lip under my top teeth. How in the hell is that thing going to fit inside me? My fevered mind is spinning with lust, anticipation, and fear.

"Someone likes what she sees," Ethan says with a boyish smile plastered on his face. That smile surprises me, since any other time he would have his arrogant I'm-all-that smirk. Did he honestly think I wouldn't like what I saw? The man is beyond gorgeous and well-endowed, and he knows it.

I'm petrified to speak since my voice may give away that I am scared shitless at the moment. I'm just thankful that he is mistaking my fear for something else entirely, so I just smile a goofy grin and nod my head. My small gesture holds more truth than not.

Ethan lies down next to me, his mouth meeting mine, our tongues dancing rhythmically. All the while, his fingers tweak at my nipples, alternating between both of my breasts. My back arches slightly from the pillows as the sensation runs from my nipples straight down to my slick, throbbing sex. Ethan's mouth leaves mine as he gently nips his way down to my needy breasts.

"Fuck, woman. I can just play with these tits all day."

The only coherent thing that I can get out of my mouth is, "Mm-hmm."

I can feel his erection pressing against my leg as he continues to work my breasts with his mouth. His right hand is tracing circles down my tight stomach and over my pubic bone. His fingers slide easily over my wetness, gently grazing my clit, and a deep groan comes to the surface from Ethan's throat. My body instantly reacts and convulses at the graze of his fingers.

"I love that you are completely bare, Lexi. This is so fucking hot, and your pussy is so wet for me," he says as he slides one finger inside me. "Oh God, you're so tight too, baby."

I suck in a breath as my body adjusts to having his finger inside me. I've been to the gynecologist, but this is obviously way different than what my doctor does.

He finger fucks me to prime me for his cock. He slides a second finger inside me as he continues to work me. His hips move in unison with his hand as he rubs his cock against my leg, his mouth kissing my neck.

"Lexi, baby, I have to have you now. I can't wait. I promise the second go-around will be everything you deserve, but right now, after all these years of waiting, I just need to be balls deep inside you and ride you hard and fast."

I know that if he does it his way, it's going to hurt like hell, but maybe that's what I need. I think of it like removing a Band-Aid—the faster you go, the less it will hurt.

"Ethan, take me however you need me."

As soon as the words leave my mouth, he pulls me down the bed a little farther, spreading my legs wider as he settles himself between my thighs. Then he reaches over to my nightstand to grab a condom. He is sheathed in latex within seconds. The bulging head of his cock rests at the entrance between my slick folds. His mouth captures mine as he begins to work his cock into my very tight virginal opening. My eyes are closed tight as I try to concentrate on relaxing, but the tinge of pain is making it difficult.

"How long has it been since you've had sex, baby? Your pussy is fighting me."

Ethan's question catches me completely off guard, so I say the first thing that comes to mind. "Don't go slow, Ethan. Just fuck me already."

That is all he needs to hear. The next thing I feel is the thrust of his hips penetrating forward in a swift, hard motion. His cock is fully buried in me balls deep, just like he wanted, and shattering me in the process. My nails dig into his back as I bite down hard onto his shoulder, trying to mask the scream of pain that wants to rip from my throat. He immediately stills, allowing my body to adjust to his invasion.

"Ah!" he yells as my teeth sink into his flesh, breaking the skin. "My girl's a biter. I love it!" he says. "Your tight little cunt feels fucking amazing. You are soaking wet," he says between panted breaths as he slowly continues to rock his hips, still allowing my body to adjust to him.

I'm pretty sure it's blood from him popping my cherry that's made me even more wet and slippery. I quickly maneuver to grab his face and pull his mouth back to mine so he doesn't look down in the middle of our fuck session, since that is exactly what this is. I don't want him to see what probably looks like a horror film between my legs.

My body is wound tight with foreign pain as Ethan proceeds to pick up his pace and work me hard. His movements are fluid and steady. Our bodies glisten with sweat. My lady bits feel like they've been shredded, even though I know that isn't the case. With every thrust of Ethan, I feel a piece of me tear away.

"Tell me what you need for you to come, baby," he pleads breathlessly as he works his cock deep inside me, his thrusts becoming more vigorous.

Since I have no clue what would make me come or help me ignore the pain factor, I simply reply, "This is all for you, Ethan. I'm all for you. I want you to come for me."

"Could you be any more perfect?" He asks the question right before his mouth latches back to mine, not waiting for an answer. The strokes of his tongue mimic the fervent thrusts of his hips.

I didn't think it was possible, but I can feel Ethan's rigid length get harder and swell bigger as he nears his release. After a few more pumps of his hips, his orgasm rips through him. A garbled version of my name with colorfully explicit words tumble incoherently from his mouth as Ethan's powerful body shudders and he empties himself inside me. His breathing is ragged as his head rests at the crook of my neck, where he is giving me featherlight kisses. We both lie there trying to calm our breathing and rapid heartbeats that pound against our chests. Once Ethan regains his composure and his body stops trembling, he pulls his semihard cock from my aching, throbbing pussy so he can go clean up.

Now comes the time to explain.

⌒☉

"Holy shit, Lexi. If you are on your period, you could have told me. I mean it wouldn't have made a difference, but I could have grabbed a towel to put down or something," Ethan says as he sees blood between my legs, on the sheets, and on his latex-covered shaft.

"I'm not on my period, Ethan. I haven't had one since I started doing the birth control shots to regulate them."

"I'm not following. Then why is there blood, and how are you not freaking out if you are not on your period?" The look on his face is of total confusion because he assumed I wasn't a virgin.

Suddenly, feelings of guilt, embarrassment, and vulnerability crash over me for not being forthcoming. I'm naked and bloody, which isn't helping the situation, so I gather my sheets and pull them to my chin before I simply answer, "Because up until roughly ten minutes ago, I was a virgin."

# Chapter Seven

"Come again?" Ethan asks.

The tension in the room is thick enough to cut with a knife. I try to lighten the mood and rid his face of its shocked expression as I tease, "Well, technically, I haven't come yet, so I can't really come again."

"Are you seriously trying to joke about this and make light of what just happened? Why didn't you tell me you were a virgin, Lexi? I would have done things very differently. Instead, you let me slam into you. Christ, I could have seriously hurt you." He runs his hands through his mussed-up hair and over his face. His expression is pained.

"I won't lie—it hurt like fucking hell, and yes, I'm sore, but I wouldn't have wanted it any other way. Feeling how much you needed me allowed me to give you what you wanted, balls deep," I say with a shrug of my shoulders.

Ethan turns, shaking his head as he stalks off toward the bathroom. I assume it's to clean up the mess that is drying on him. After a few moments, I hear the shower turn on, and it surprises me when he comes back into the room, still gloriously naked, less the condom, and he's carrying a cup in his hand.

"Here's some ibuprofen to help alleviate some of the pain," he says, handing me the pills and the water. Once I've taken the pills, he asks,

"Come shower with me?"

I nod, take the hand he offers to help me out of bed, and follow him to my bathroom. We both step into the shower, and I find myself immediately engulfed in an affectionate embrace as he places a kiss at the top of my head. We stay like that for a few minutes before he releases his hold on me and begins to lather my body with soap. He is extremely gentle as his hands work the tenderness between my thighs. It's actually kind of sweet that he is taking care of me in such an intimate manner after fucking me. Once Ethan has thoroughly washed my body, he begins massaging shampoo into my hair. His hands feel amazing on my scalp as he works the shampoo, followed by conditioner. As soon as he is done bathing me, he quickly washes himself, using my fruit-scented body wash. The scent contradicts his manliness, but I don't care since I finally get a chance to admire the fine form of Ethan Gage as his muscles flex with every movement as he washes himself.

I can't help that my eyes wander south below his torso, and even though Ethan is flaccid, his penis is still impressively perfect. The right side of his mouth quirks up in a smirk as he catches my wandering eyes roaming over his body. For once I'm not embarrassed that I was caught taking in the sight before me. He's perfection, and right now, he's all mine.

Ethan turns to shut off the water once he's rinsed off and steps from the shower, turning back to hand me my robe off the hook before he grabs a towel to dry himself off. I slide my arms into the sleeves and loosely tie the belt around my waist.

I occasionally glance at Ethan's reflection in the mirror as he watches me comb out the knots in my hair with my wide-tooth comb before I pile the wet mess on top of my head with a large clip. His arms are crossed over his chest, and he's watching me intently. There is no modesty with this man, as he only wears the towel wrapped around his hips.

Neither of us has said a single word since he asked me to shower with him. I figured I would give him the chance to absorb the bomb I dropped on him so he can come to terms with taking my virginity. Most guys would chomp at the bit to take a girl's virginity, be the first one to ever go there, but for some reason, I sense this is really bothering Ethan. I see the cogs turning in his brain, the internal struggle he seems to be having but since he isn't speaking I have not a clue as to why he's so troubled.

As I pass him to walk out of the bathroom, I place my hand on his lower back and lightly brush my lips across his tense shoulder. His entire body stiffens with my actions, and I feel a ping of hurt shoot through my chest as I exit the bathroom, leaving him alone with his thoughts.

Once I've changed into a pair of leggings with a purple-and-white tunic, I step from my closet to find him fully dressed, sitting on the edge of my bed with his elbows resting on top of his knees, hands locked together, and head down. The desperate need to break this deafening silence is overwhelming.

"Hey, are you OK?" I finally ask.

His head slowly comes up, and his haunted eyes meet mine. My heart aches when all I see is regret swimming in the pools of gray.

"Why didn't you tell me?"

"Would it have really made a difference, Ethan? What is going on in that head of yours? Your eyes tell me you regret what just happened. Please don't ruin this special day for me," I plead.

Ethan's eyes never leave mine, but he still hasn't answered my questions. I watch his jaw clench and the vein in his neck pulse as he is carefully considering what his next words will be. I slowly cross the room toward him. His hands separate, allowing me access to step between his legs. He wraps his arms around my waist and lowers his forehead to my sternum, inhaling a deep breath. I cradle his head, kissing the top, silently willing him to speak. I was being honest when I told him I wouldn't have wanted him any other way, and this silence is killing me.

"I'm sorry," I whisper. I'm at a complete disadvantage here, and I don't know what else to say.

He pulls back, looking at me like I just grew a second head before finally speaking. "Why are you apologizing to me? I should be apologizing to you. I'm sorry for how this all went down. I would have never taken you like that if I knew this was your first time."

"Dammit, Ethan! What more can I say? Or better yet, how can I show you that I really am OK with this? I don't regret how we had sex or having sex period. I just hope that you don't regret it either." Tears burn the back of my throat.

"Baby, I would never regret what you just gave me. It was just a shock; that's all. You are a smart, gorgeous, and kind woman, and I've assumed that some lucky bastard already got that gift. I truly am thankful that I'm the lucky bastard." Sincerity dances through his stormy eyes.

Ethan stands, cupping my face in his hands as he dips his head to place a delicate kiss on my lips. He moves his hands to the hem of my tunic, and with one swift motion, my top is removed, leaving my bare breasts exposed. Ethan's mouth latches to my right nipple. Instantly, my head falls back, my eyes close, and a moan slips from my lips as he teases the bud, alternating between nips of his teeth and soft circles with his heated tongue. I feel wetness pool between my thighs from my arousal. His hands quickly remove the leggings I am wearing as he slowly lays me back onto my bed with my legs hanging over the edge. Ethan stands straight, taking in the sight of my naked body. Another one of his sexy-as-hell primal growls of appreciation erupts from his throat. He discards his clothes as quickly as he had taken off mine, his cock standing erect and beautiful. I imagine it to feel like silk inside my mouth. I would love to run my tongue along the shaft before taking him in my mouth and swallowing him whole.

He bends at the waist, placing light kisses between my breasts and down the length of my torso toward my slick sex. His tongue draws languid circles over my pubic bone, and my hips writhe from the tingling sensation. Ethan kneels down on the floor between my legs. He places each one of my feet on the edge of my bed, spreading my legs farther apart as he runs his nose up my glistening seam, inhaling a breath as he does so.

"You smell fucking amazing, baby. I'm going to eat you until you come, and then I'm going to eat you until you come again."

My body shivers with anticipation. "I don't care what you do as long as you touch me, Ethan," I say through panting breaths.

"Slow and easy this time, baby. I want you to enjoy this."

His expert tongue gently licks at my opening. My hips buck on their own, forcing Ethan to place a hand on my lower abdomen in an effort to hold me down. The fingers on his free hand spread my tender flesh, allowing his tongue full access to thrust inside my swollen pussy, lapping up the juices of my arousal. My back arches, my eyes screw shut, and his name is but a whisper from my lips as my hands fist into his hair, holding his head firmly in place.

"Oh. My. God. Ethan," I pant out as I feel a tightening sensation building in my core. "Don't stop."

I feel a slight grin from his lips as he continues the assault on my quivering sex. He inserts a finger, crooked slightly to rub the hypersensitive tissues of my G-spot, as his tongue circles vigorously over my clit. Everything inside me heats up to inferno temperatures as my core winds even tighter, and as if the world speeds up into hyperdrive, my body explodes in the most delicious way. "Holy hell, Ethan!" I scream as my mind whirls off into oblivion as the earthshattering orgasm rakes through my body in pure ecstasy.

Ethan swiftly moves from the floor, gently pulling me farther up my bed as he lies down next to me. My entire body is sensitive and sweaty. I roll to my side so I am facing him, looking deep into the sexually driven storm thundering in his eyes. He captures my mouth in a tender yet succulent kiss. My orgasm is present on his lips, but I honestly don't care about anything at this moment other than Ethan Gage's naked body next to me.

"You taste divine, Miss Morgan," he mumbles, inevitably making my cheeks blush crimson with his comment.

"You, Mr. Gage, are absolutely wonderful," I say sleepily.

"Are you hungry, babe?"

"Hmm?"

"Sleep, my beautiful girl," he whispers, kissing my forehead.

# Chapter Eight

I wake suddenly, dripping in sweat, my heart beating erratically against my chest. My room is pitch-black, and all I hear is the blood pounding in my ears. I sit up, reaching for the light on my nightstand. I pull my knees to my chest as I think about the nightmare that invaded my sleep.

My dream was of the early morning after the big earthquake that just shook the Bay Area. My body was slowly walking down a long, sterile hallway lit with horrible, flickering fluorescent lighting. The man I was following was wearing a white doctor's coat that looked to be a little too long, with buttons that were stressed in the front from his overly large gut. He was shorter than I was with a heavily round build and a bald spot on the crown of his head. This squat of a man was leading me toward the morgue where my parents' bodies were brought after the accident that claimed their lives. He slid his badge to unlock the double doors and held one side open for me to walk inside. As I passed him to enter, I could smell the stench of stale cigarette smoke on him. That one whiff was enough to make my stomach churn.

The room was chilled and reeked of heavy-duty cleaning chemicals and I didn't want to know what else. My body was shaking from nerves and the eeriness of the room. My eyes immediately went to the only two sterile rolling tables that had covered bodies lying on them. All I could see were the feet with toe tags. The man walked to the nearest table and was standing next to it, asking if I was ready to view the body. Just as I shook my head, he flung back the sheet. I screamed, covering my eyes, and that was when I jerked awake from the hellish nightmare.

A feverish chill rolls down my spine at the remembrance of that fateful morning. I'm trying to shake off the sensation of loneliness the dream has left me feeling when I realize that I am alone. Ethan is no longer in my bed with me.

I swing my legs over the edge, grab my leggings and tunic from the floor, and dress quickly. His clothes are gone, so I can only assume he dressed and is somewhere in my house. I cross to my bathroom, flipping on the light so I can brush my teeth. Once I'm finished, I head downstairs to see if Ethan is in the kitchen or family room, but I already know he's not in either since the lights are off. I turn on the kitchen light and look out into the darkened backyard, lit only by moonlight, and he's not out there either. "Where did he go?" I whisper to myself.

Before I head back to my room, I grab a bottled water from the refrigerator, downing half of it before making it back to my room. My alarm clock shows that it's just after three in the morning. I go to my French doors and glance over at Ethan's house only to find that his R8 is no longer in the driveway. What the fuck? Where the hell did he go, and why didn't he wake me before he left? I go back downstairs to check the front door, and it was left unlocked, so I lock it again. If he ran out for something, then he can ring the doorbell when he returns.

I crawl back into bed, and that is when I see a handwritten note on the pillow Ethan had been sleeping on.

*Alexa—*
*You are forever mine. Do not forget that.*
*EG*

Those few words are all that he wrote on my stationary, and I have no idea what he means by them. I grab my cell phone and type out a text in hopes he will answer.

Me: Hey. I woke & you were gone. Where'd you go?

I turn off my light on the nightstand and settle back in bed, waiting for a response.

# Chapter Nine

My alarm clock sounds at six thirty, beckoning me to wake up. I smack my hand down to stop its whining and grab my cell phone to see if Ethan ever replied. He didn't. A whole ball of insecurities roll through my stomach, and my chest feels tight. Why wouldn't he text me back? Everything seemed perfect when I fell asleep in his arms after my mind-blowing orgasm. I thought I would take a quick nap, and then he would wake me to have his wicked way with me again, this time slow and easy. Apparently, I was wrong.

As I pass my French doors to go get ready for school, I glance over to see the empty driveway of Ethan's house. I shake my head and continue to the bathroom. I quickly shower, because if I stand in there too long, my mind will wander to the very intimate shower I had with Ethan yesterday, and I need to focus on what today will entail, not on Ethan Gage.

I'm ready within an hour, and I grab my sugar-free Red Bull from the refrigerator before heading to the garage. When I step inside, I see my dad's car parked next to mine, and I freeze, sucking in a deep breath. Keep it together, Lexi. Keep it together. Just get through today. That is all I can tell myself right now. I pass the Audi and get into my car. I take a few steadying breaths before pulling out of the garage and heading to school.

I pull into the school parking lot, and the twins are waving at me to park next to them, so I do. I gather my stuff from the passenger seat and barely clear the car before I am immediately grabbed in a three-way hug with Jessa and Becca. Everything I had in my arms has fallen to the ground, but I needed this from two of my best friends. I struggle to keep my tears at bay, but it's a battle that I lose.

They pull away, and Becca bends down to grab my belongings to hand back to me.

"Thanks," I say in a low, shaky voice.

"We love you, bitch," Jessa says in a somber tone.

"I love you, skanks," I say with a forced smile. I swipe away my tears and regain my composure. I really need to try to keep it together today.

The twins say nothing more as we start to head across the parking lot toward the school entrance. Other students are passing by. Some stare, and some just glance quickly and keep going. I'm sure everyone has an idea as to what has happened and is probably shocked that I'm here, but I can't fall behind in school for fear of losing my place at Stanford. Plus, school will help keep my mind occupied and off of disappearing Ethan.

We approach the steps and see Principal Cassidy standing at the top, looking down in my direction with sympathy gleaming in her eyes. She's young for a principal, maybe in her early to midforties. Mrs. Cassidy is a petite woman with naturally curly chestnut hair that falls just below her shoulders. Her eyes are dark brown with speckles of gold, giving them warmth. It's not often students like their principals, but Principal Cassidy is loved by all of her students. It wouldn't surprise me if she knew all fifteen hundred-plus of us by name, since she's very personable like that.

"Miss Morgan. May I speak to you privately in my office?" she asks as we get closer.

"Of course, Principal Cassidy," I reply and then glance over at the twins and tell them I will see them in a bit.

Both girls nod and then wave hello to Principal Cassidy.

"Good morning, ladies," she responds with a smile.

I walk next to Principal Cassidy through the main hallway while other students whisper and stare as we pass by. You would think I grew a third arm instead of having my parents die unexpectedly three days ago. Once we reach her office, she closes the door behind her.

"Please have a seat, Alexa," she says, gesturing to one of the leather chairs that faces her large walnut desk.

I place my backpack, purse, and a couple of books that wouldn't fit in my backpack onto the second chair before taking my seat.

"Is something wrong, Mrs. Cassidy?" I ask warily.

"Not at all, Alexa. First and foremost, I want to give you my condolences. It's never easy losing a parent, but you have lost both at the same time, and I can only imagine the devastation you have endured already. I'm actually surprised to see you here today."

"I felt it was necessary. Even though I just received my early acceptance letter to Stanford, I cannot afford to fall behind," I respond simply.

"Congratulations, young lady. That is wonderful news," she says as pride flashes in her kind eyes. "With that being said, I would like to offer you this week and next week to take care of your personal obligations. I have already spoken with your teachers, and they are all understanding and very much willing to give you your assignments in advance. This way, you won't fall behind. They have also offered that any assignment that requires your teacher's assistance, they will make themselves available to you through a web-based meeting or the phone."

"I don't know what to say. I really do appreciate what you are offering. Later today will be my first real day of this new reality, since

I have to start handling funeral arrangements." My voice cracks as I fight back the tears.

"Go home, Alexa. I will have your teachers e-mail you your assignments by the end of the day. Please call me if you need anything or would like some help. Here," Principal Cassidy says with a caring smile that reaches her eyes as she hands me a Post-it with her home and cell phone numbers written in perfect penmanship.

"Thank you, Principal Cassidy," I say as I stand, tucking her phone number into my pocket, and grab the stuff I placed on the other chair.

"I mean it, Alexa. Call me if you need anything."

I smile back over my shoulder as I exit her office. The hallways are quiet since the bell rang and the students are in class now. It makes the trip out to my car a lot faster. Once I'm in it, I inhale a huge breath and will myself to keep it together until I get home. I take out my phone and quickly type a text to the twins, letting them know I am heading home and will talk to them later. After a couple of messages back and forth, we end our chat. I then send Devin a text.

Me: Hey. Are you in class?
Devin: Nah. I have a free period 1st period.
Me: My principal is letting me do my school work from home for the next 2 wks. Heading home now.
Devin: I'll see you in an hour.
Me: What? You have class.
Devin: I will get my assignments. See you in an hour.
Me: Thx Dev.
Devin: Anytime Lex.

⤶

I'm lounging out by the pool reading a book on my Kindle when Devin texts me to say he's at the front door. I get up, placing my Kindle on the table next to the chaise lounge, and head inside to open the door for Devin.

Devin is standing on the stoop wearing blue, gray, and white plaid shorts with a simple blue T-shirt and flip-flops, and his sandy-blond hair has the messy bedhead look. He has his backpack slung over one shoulder, a suitcase on wheels stands beside him, and a large duffel bag lies at his feet. I can't help but smile at the sight before me.

"Hey," I say, opening the door wider. I bend down and grab his duffel bag so Devin can step inside the door with his suitcase in tow.

"Hey, yourself." He smiles. "Where do you want me?"

"Let's drop your stuff in the first room up the stairs to the right. Then we can have lunch while we sit outside until your parents get here."

"I almost forgot they were coming over later. I guess the handle of Jack that I brought will have to wait," he says with a devilishly handsome grin.

My left eyebrow arches at his statement. "So that's why your duffel bag weighs so much. Well, I'm sure I'm going to need a shot or three after I sit with your parents. This evening is not going to be easy for any of us," I say as we head up the stairs to put his bags in the spare room.

Once we drop the bags on the bed, we head back downstairs to the kitchen so I can make us a couple of sandwiches. We grab our plates and then go downstairs and out the back slider. Once we set our plates on the table between the lounges, Devin envelopes me in his arms, hugging me tight and placing a kiss at my temple. It feels so good being in his strong arms. I needed him to be here, and he dropped everything to be with me.

Devin and I sit on lounge chairs taking in the late-morning sunshine. It's a little cooler outside than the previous days, but it's perfect for this time of year. Our conversation mostly consists of school, plans for senior year, and what we want to do once we start Stanford next August. I am beyond happy he will be at Stanford with me. It's a large campus, and the chances of running into each other will be slim unless we plan it, but I hope to have at least one or two classes with him since we both need to complete our general education before focusing on our prerequisites for our chosen majors.

"So what will your major be, Dev?" I ask since I have no clue.

"I thought about sport medicine, but the chance to work for a professional team is slim, so I decided to major in civil and environmental engineering," he answers. "Stanford has an excellent program for it, and California has plenty of career opportunities in that field once I graduate. Plus, I wouldn't be stuck at a desk all day, and the thought of being outside for work is appealing."

"Well, I'm glad you didn't say 'I don't know' and hope to become the next awesome quarterback for the 49ers," I tease.

"Oh, don't get me wrong. If the 49ers approached me, I would be all over it." He laughs, winking at me.

Devin truly is amazing, and I'm surprised some lucky girl hasn't snatched him up. I guess, in a strange way, I'm glad he doesn't have a girlfriend. He wouldn't be here with me if he did, as I'm sure she wouldn't understand our relationship, since most females are the jealous type.

"Hey, I have to take off for a couple of hours tomorrow. Will you be OK alone?" he asks.

"Of course I will be OK. I can knock out some of my homework. It's nice that I will have two weeks' worth of assignments sent all at once so I can try and get it done sooner rather than later and concentrate on the shit storm that is headed my way. That is unless you want me to go with you."

"Nah, I just have a couple of errands to take care of."

"OK."

We decide to go into the hot tub for a little while, so we just shuck our clothes like last time. No sense in wasting time changing into swimsuits since undergarments cover the same territory. Our conversation comes easily as we joke with each other. Devin's facial expression changes slightly, like he's thinking about something.

"Penny for your thoughts." I smile.

"Will I be blessed with your douche bag neighbor's presence? I don't want to argue; I just want to be prepared if he shows."

Since I've never been good at lying or hiding things, I just tell Devin the truth. "No, you won't be seeing him. I haven't seen or heard from him since yesterday after we slept together. He only left a cryptic note on my pillow."

Devin's body tenses since I just told him I slept with Ethan. Anger then hurt flashes through his sea of blues. I feel like shit for telling him this way, but I knew it would come up again eventually and I would rather have no secrets between us.

"Do you love him, Lexi?"

"Love him, no. I lusted for him. I guess with everything that is going on, I just needed to feel something more than emotional pain, and he was a strong enough presence since the earthquake. I don't regret what I did, even though in my mind, I guess he finally got what he wanted and then left me sometime in the night."

"Motherfucker! He really just left you in the middle of the night?"

"Pretty much," I answer with a shrug.

"What did the note say? Never mind. You don't have to tell me."

"It's fine. It said something about always being his." I wait a second before I continue, "Dev, I gave him my virginity." I whisper the last part, trying to hold back the tears that are beginning to blur my vision. I wipe the single tear that escapes, frustrated, as I tell him, "The note is confusing, and I really don't want to hate him or regret what I've done.

For now, he's gone, he hasn't even tried to get ahold of me, and I don't know if he will ever come back."

Devin doesn't say anything. I wonder if he even heard me say the part about my virginity. He slides closer to me and pulls me into a half hug, since a full hug is awkward the way we are sitting in the hot tub. He kisses my temple before releasing me. His deep blue eyes stare into my honey-brown ones with undeniable love. I blush at the way his eyes give away every emotion and the feelings he has for me. I'm pretty sure my eyes do the same. I was never good at hiding my feelings either.

My phone chimes with a text message, and I glance at the screen. Marie Miller is shown on the display. I swipe the phone alive, read the text, and then reply to her quickly.

"Your parents are on their way. Should we just order pizza for dinner? It will be close to five thirty by the time they get across the bridge."

"Pizza sounds good. Plus, we can have leftovers later once we get our buzz on," he says with a mischievous grin.

"I almost forgot about that," I say, bumping shoulders with him. "I guess we should shower and get dressed since your parents are on their way."

Devin hops out of the hot tub, holding a hand out to help me. I grab his hand, and he pulls me out of the tub and into his lean, chiseled body. I make an "oomph" sound when our bodies collide. He gives me a half smile as his arms tighten a little more around my waist. My pulse is racing, and for the first time ever, I want Devin to kiss me. He leans down like he's going to, but his lips graze my forehead lightly. A wave of disappointment courses through me as I lay my head against his chest. His hold loosens, and then he finally releases me. He bends down, collecting the clothing we shed by the hot tub. We walk into the house and upstairs to shower.

I walk over to the linen closet in the hallway and hand Devin a towel and washcloth. "This bathroom is all yours." I nod toward the guest bath at the end of the hall. "I'll see you in a few," I say as I head to my bedroom, closing the double doors behind me.

I pass the French doors to my balcony and see a limousine parked in front of Ethan's house. I watch briefly and see Olivia and Victor Gage emerge from the car while the driver unloads a massive amount of luggage from the trunk. I guess they're back from Europe.

I continue into my bathroom so I can wash the smell of chlorine off of my skin. As I'm scrubbing my body with my loofa, I talk myself into going over to the Gages' and asking if they know where Ethan is. I just want to know that he's OK. At least that's what I keep telling myself. I wasn't lying to Devin when I said I didn't want to regret what happened yesterday. I hastily rinse the suds off and dry my body. I go into my closet and throw on a pair of skinny jeans, an off-the-shoulder T-shirt, and my flip-flops.

When I step out of my room, Devin is walking toward his room with just a towel wrapped around his waist. His hair is still damp, hanging just above his brow line. His athletic body still has a slight sheen to it. My breath hitches at the sight of him. He is simply gorgeous.

"Where you headed, Lex?" Devin asks with a raised eyebrow.

"Umm, I'm just going to run over to the Gages' really quick. They just got home from a vacation. Could you order the pizza? The number is on the fridge," I say hastily.

Devin's eyes narrow, but he is wise not to say anything about where I'm going. He nods, silently saying that he will order the pizza. I start to walk away but turn and hug him before I head down the stairs and out the front door.

It feels strange walking over to Ethan's house knowing he isn't there and also because of the fact that I have never gone over in all the years we have been neighbors. I stop for a second in front of the house that separates our homes. My nerves are starting to get the best of me, and my feet are frozen in place. Why am I scared? Shake it off and move your ass, Lex. I will my feet to continue forward, and they finally obey my silent plea and start to move. Thank God!

I walk up to the double doors and barely tap on the door. No one is going to hear that wimpy knock, Lexi. I reach up to knock a little louder when the door swings open, startling me and apparently Victor Gage as well.

"Alexa, what a surprise," he says with a smile. "I'm so sorry to hear about your parents. If you need anything, please do not hesitate to ask me or Olivia. We would love to help you any way we can."

"Um, thank you, Victor. That is very thoughtful of you." His condolences catch me off guard. I guess Ethan must have explained to his parents what had transpired after the earthquake.

A woman's elegant voice calls out, "Vic, honey, who are you talking to?"

"Alexa is at the door."

Olivia Gage rounds the corner with a look I do not recognize. It almost resembles jealousy, which would be strange. Her eyes then lighten to what now looks like sympathy. "Oh, Lexi. We are so terribly sorry to hear about your parents." She steps closer to give me a hug. Her body is tense and cold. There is nothing warm or comforting about the embrace. It sends a chill down my spine.

Stepping back to distance myself, I say, "Thank you, Olivia. I appreciate the support your family has offered me. That is actually why I'm here. I haven't seen Ethan since yesterday, and he's been really good about checking on me since all of this happened. Do you happen to know where he is?"

Olivia looks at me with tension etched around her eyes. I can see that she is trying to gather her thoughts before finally answering, "He's in Seattle, dear. He was supposed to be there Friday night, but with everything that occurred, we told him he had until Sunday night to get there. We knew we would be home today, and I promised him that I would keep a close eye on you. He has been very concerned about you." She eyes me suspiciously, making me feel uncomfortable.

"Seattle? He never mentioned anything to me over the last couple of days."

"He will be up there for the next eight months or so to watch over the renovations of our new northwest offices," Victor answers.

"Oh. OK. Well, I'm glad nothing bad has happened to him or that he just disappeared, then." My reply is weak with an even weaker smile.

"Is there anything we can help you with, dear?" Olivia asks.

"No. I'm OK. My parents' best friends are on their way over to help me plan the funeral. Thank you again for the offer. I guess I will let you both get to unpacking. I'm sure you have a lot to do," I say as I step away.

"We'll see you later, Lexi," Olivia says icily as she closes the door. Just as I step off their porch, I hear her yell something at Victor and a plea from him for her to calm down. What the hell?

I head back to my house, trying to figure out why Ethan never said anything to me about Seattle. I'm sure he has his reasons, and, unfortunately, I will never be privy to them.

# Chapter Ten

George and Marie have been at the house for nearly two hours when we finalize a plan for my parents' ashes. Earlier in the day, George reached out to my parents' lawyer to ask if there was anything in writing stating what should be done in the case that one or both of them were deceased. Mr. Rocklin faxed George the page that clearly stated that neither parent wanted to be buried or kept in a mausoleum and that I can do what I would like with their ashes. We were able to arrange for my parents' bodies to be cremated in two days. Once I take possession of the ashes, I will hold a small remembrance at the house for close friends and business partners. It's always been just the three of us, so we have no living relatives to invite. The instructions also clearly state that their lives should be honored with a party and not a depressing funeral, so that is exactly what I will do. I will throw them a party they would have been proud of.

"Alexa, Mr. Rocklin would like to meet with you to go over Joseph and Jeanine's wills and your trust on Wednesday. Please give him a call tomorrow to confirm a time," George advises me.

"I'll call tomorrow to confirm. Thank you for getting this part of the document. I really appreciate it." I smile and give George a half hug.

"We will always be here for you, Alexa, no matter what," Marie says with more tears sliding down her cheeks.

We all stand from the dining table, stretching since we've been sitting there for so long.

"I know you will be. That's what is keeping me together right now. You are the only family I have left, and you're not even blood." My voice trembles as I choke back a sob.

Devin steps behind me and wraps his arms around my shoulders when he addresses his parents. "I'm gonna stay here with Lex for a couple of days. I'm cleared with school and have all my assignments."

"What about football practice, son?" George asks.

"Coach is good with me missing a few days. I'm still playing in the game Saturday. Hopefully I can drag this one so she can see how awesome I am," he says as he rocks me side to side.

"Of course I will go, Dev." I tilt my head to see his face and smile up at him.

"All right, then. Your mother and I have an early day tomorrow, so I guess we should hit the road. You two stay out of trouble," George says with laughter in his voice.

"But of course, Father," Devin teases back as he releases me. He quickly turns to capture his mom in a big hug, and I hear him whisper, "I love you, Mom."

Marie replies, "Love you too, my not so baby boy," as more tears trickle down her cheeks.

"Drive safe, you two," I say as they head out the door.

"Always do," George hollers over his shoulder.

I close and lock the front door once I see the Millers' taillights heading down the street. I turn, but Devin isn't behind me anymore.

"So how about those shots?" I yell to nowhere in particular, since I don't know where he went.

"I'm already ahead of ya." He beams as he appears from the guest room and comes back down the stairs with the bottle of Jack in his hand.

126

"That you are."

We head down to the bar, where I grab a couple of shot glasses so Devin can pour the shots.

"Cheers to good company after a shitty day," he says.

"I'll drink to that," I say as we clank shot glasses. We both do our shots like pros. This drinking business is getting a little too easy. Once everything settles a little bit, I won't drink anymore. Well, at least not until I'm in college. I have to be careful since I have way too much to lose if I become an alcoholic. Addiction runs in my blood, since my biological mother was an alcoholic and heroin addict. I definitely do not want to be like her, ever.

I am thankful when my phone chimes with a text message. I need to get out of my head and away from the horrible thoughts of my biological mother. I grab the phone from my back pocket to see that it's Becca.

Becca: Hey bitch. Just checking on you. Want some company?
Me: Thanks skank. I'm ok. Devin is here with me.
Becca: Devin? Mr. Invisible for the past 2 yrs must be making up for lost time.
Me: It's all good right now. I promise I will let you & J know what's going on in the next couple of days. I have to meet with the lawyer on Wed.
Becca: Ok. Luvs ya. XO
Me: Luvs ya more.

Devin has thoughtfully poured us each another shot. We toss them back, and I catch a flash of uncertainty flicker through his vibrant blue eyes, like he is contemplating something, before he finally asks, "So did you find out where he is?"

"Yeah, he's in Seattle looking over the Gages' new northwest office renovation. Apparently he didn't think to tell me this information while he was still here and before he—" I stop myself because I know Devin doesn't need to hear it again.

"So he's not dead and there's really no good explanation for not contacting you other than he's a total fucktard?"

"That pretty much sums it up." I shrug as I turn to head up to the kitchen to grab a couple of beers from the refrigerator. When I come back down, Devin is smiling from ear to ear with a shot in each hand. I've never noticed before, but he has the slightest dimple in his left cheek that seems to only appear when he genuinely smiles this amazing smile I've never been blessed with in all the years we've known each other.

I set the beers on top of the bar so we can do our third shot. Once we slam our shot glasses down, Devin grabs the beers, twists the caps off, and hands me mine while he takes a tug from his own bottle. Staring at the guy in front of me, I just smile at him and think about how lucky I am and how comfortable it is to have him here. If he weren't here right now, I would most likely be holed up in my bedroom, a blubbering mess over the death of my parents and the crazy confusing couple of days with Ethan.

"What's that look for, Lex?" Devin asks, because I assume I have some strange look plastered on my face.

"Oh, nothing. I was just thinking of how lucky I am to have you back in my life," I answer honestly.

"I'm the lucky one. I don't think I would have been so forgiving if the tables were turned and you walked away from me two years ago."

"That's done and over with, Dev. Let's not dwell on things we can't change. Going forward, we will not speak of those two years, OK?"

"Deal," he says, holding out his fist for me to bump. I oblige, as this was our thing we used to do so many years ago. This one little action sends us both into a fit of laughter. "Damn, we are dumb," he says as he laughs harder.

"What do you say to doing one more shot, grabbing another beer, and heading to my room so we can watch *A Nightmare on Elm Street*?"

"I say that sounds perfect."

⌒♄

*I'm back in the morgue, and the creepy doctor is standing at the head of one of the tables with his hand on the sheet. He asks if I'm ready to view the body, and just as I shake my head, he pulls the sheet back. I scream, covering my eyes because I'm not ready to see the body that lies beneath the sheet. I keep my eyes screwed shut, chanting over and over for him to cover the body. I feel something shaking me as I keep repeating the chant. Then I hear a voice, but my own words are drowning it out. Suddenly, my eyes open wide to a dimly lit room as I try to catch my breath and get my bearings straight. Once I realize I'm in the safety of my room, I sit up quickly, reaching for my nightstand light. It takes a moment for my eyes to adjust to the brightness, but when they do, I look over to see Devin's face etched with concern.*

"You're OK, Lexi. You were having a nightmare," he says in a tone to soothe me. He scoots closer and wraps one arm around my shoulders, pulling me into the side of his body so he can chase away the horrible dream. "I was trying to wake you, but you kept saying to cover the body and you couldn't hear my voice."

"Oh God, Dev. It was horrible. Having to identify my parents' bodies was the hardest thing I ever had to do. I would never wish that upon my greatest enemy. The room was cold and sterile with a god-awful smell. The doctor was so creepy, like right out of a scary movie, and he didn't even give me a chance to prepare myself. I hated every second of it, and now their mangled images are forever branded in my mind. I can never unsee that." My voice garbles as tears stream down my face, and sobs begin to rake over my body.

"Sh, it will be OK." Devin is rubbing his hand up and down my arm, holding me close.

I stay in Devin's comforting hold for a while. My sobs have turned to hiccups, and my nose has run all down the front of Devin's shirt. He has tearstains on his chest. My TV loops the DVD home screen over and over until I pull away, grabbing the remote off of my nightstand and turning it off.

"I'm sorry, Dev. Your shirt is a mess because of me," I offer as a pathetic apology.

"Don't be sorry. I'm glad I'm here to give you some sort of security," he says as he removes his snotty T-shirt. "Do you need to blow your nose?" he teases with a slight smile.

"Very funny, but yes," I say as I snag the shirt from him and proceed to blow my nose with it. The sound that comes out is like a goose honk and is very unladylike.

"Now that right there is sexy," he says, laughing at me.

"Oh God, shut up, Dev," I say as I try to push him over but fail to even budge him.

Something changes in this moment between Devin and me. I'm not exactly sure where these sudden feelings come from, but I lunge at Devin quickly, crashing our mouths together. It's not sexy or pretty; our teeth smack together clumsily at the first connection, but it only takes seconds for our tongues to find their rhythm. A low moan vibrates through Devin's chest. I love the way his lips feel against mine. I remember loving how they felt two years ago but had to stop it. Tonight, I will not stop it, since I made the move. I know what you are thinking, that I'm a slut, but this, with Devin, is right and I need and want to keep feeling.

Devin moves to lay me back down on the bed. His body partially covers mine as our mouths make slow love to each other. My body tingles with each caress of his tongue. His hand rests on my hip. This kiss is mind-blowing. I'm lost in the passion and love that exudes off of Devin.

He pulls back, looking down into my eyes with a boyish grin playing across his lips. "Wow. I have waited for you to kiss me like that for so long," Devin says through panted breaths.

"That was incredibly—I don't even have a word to finish that compliment, Dev. Your kiss speaks volumes," I say as I place a hand to his cheek. Devin turns his head slightly to kiss the inside of my palm, sending a shock straight to my heart.

The blue pools of Devin's eyes darken just before he lowers his mouth to take mine again. I can't help but compare the difference in the kisses between Devin and Ethan. Ethan's kisses were demanding, devouring, and possessive. His were always as if he was staking claim on me, my mouth, and my body. Devin's kisses are tender, gentle, and full of love. It is night and day and leaves me in a confused haze. I squeeze out the thoughts of Ethan so I can concentrate on the here and now. I want to accept Devin's soft lips making me feel like I'm the only woman in the world for him.

I pull back to come up for air. Our breaths are pants of passion. Devin looks into my honey-brown eyes before asking, "Are you OK, Lex?"

"I'm perfect in this moment with you, Dev," I answer honestly with a smile of admiration on my lips.

Devin smiles at my response, placing a kiss to my forehead as he pulls me into his arms. "It's late, Lex. We should get some sleep. I have to get up early and take care of my errands."

I snuggle into his chest, listening to his heartbeat. It's comforting and eases any anxiety I felt earlier from the nightmare. I place a kiss to his bare chest. "Good night, Dev." My eyes feel heavy as sleep drags me under.

# Chapter Eleven

It's early Tuesday morning, and Devin has left to run whatever errands he needed to this morning. I decide to go out on my balcony to do my calculus homework. I have my morning staple of sugar-free Red Bull to help get my mind into the grueling homework that was e-mailed over to me yesterday. It's chilly this morning, but I welcome the feel of the crisp air.

I glance over at the Gage house and see a silhouette in Ethan's room. It gives me an eerie feeling, since I know he is in Seattle for the next eight months. I feel the eyes watching me. I'm not sure if it's Victor or Olivia, but whoever it is, I don't like them spying on me, so I gather my things and go back into my room to do my homework at my desk.

A few hours go by before my phone starts ringing, startling me. It's a number I don't recognize, but I can't ignore the call either.

"This is Lexi," I greet the caller when I swipe to answer the call.

"Hi, Alexa. This is Mr. Rocklin, your parents' attorney."

My blood drains instantly from my face as I am constantly reminded of what the days to come will demand from me. "Oh. Hello, Mr. Rocklin. I was meaning to call you earlier, but I got wrapped up in my homework. What time would you like me to come to your office tomorrow?"

"I'm so sorry we will have to meet under such sad circumstances.

Your parents were wonderful people, and I know they loved you very much. This is never easy, but I know you will get through it. Now, with my condolences out of the way, will nine o'clock work for you? There is a lot to cover."

"Nine will be fine. Could you please e-mail me your address? Do you need my e-mail address?"

"No. I have it, Alexa. I will send the address and instructions on what I will need you to bring with you. I will see you tomorrow at nine."

"Bye, Mr. Rocklin," I say before I hit end.

I take a deep breath after I hang up to help steady my nerves. I hate this. I hate everything about this. I want to curl up in my dad's lap like I used to when I was a little girl and have him tell me everything will be OK. I want him to chase away the pain and fear I have dwelling inside of me—something only a dad, a daughter's hero, can do for her. But that won't happen. My dad, my hero, can't chase away my pain anymore.

A strangled sob releases from my throat. I can't be strong anymore. My body is exhausted from fighting the despair. I need to cry. I need to grieve. My body convulses as the heartache registers. Tears flow freely as the dam officially breaks. I stumble to my bed and lie down, clutching onto one of my pillows as if it were my lifeline, and just let myself cry. I finally let the pain takeover. Why? Why did this happen to me? I just want my mom and dad back. Fuck my life!

*It's cold and the smell of the dimly lit room is unbearable. I'm standing with my eyes screwed tight, not wanting to look at what's beneath the white sheet. The agonizing fear has a strong hold on me when I hear the creepy doctor's voice telling me I need to identify the bodies. I've turned*

*my head and finally forced my eyes to open, still not looking directly at the table in front of me. My breathing is shallow, almost nonexistent. You have to do this, Lex. You can do this. You can't leave until you do. I slowly bring my eyes up the length of the body lying before me. When I finally look at the revealed portion of the corpse, my stomach churns and I run to the large steel sink in the room and begin vomiting viciously. Between the heaving, I yell at the doctor to cover my dad's mangled body. I know it's my dad even though his handsome features are not present. My body continues convulsing. I'm shaking uncontrollably. The shaking doesn't cease. I hear a voice calling my name, but I'm frozen in this moment.*

"Lexi, wake up, baby. Come on, Lex, wake up for me." Devin's frantic voice finally breaks through the nightmare as he is shaking my shoulders in an effort to wake me.

As if it's déjà vu all over again, my eyes open, and I dart up struggling for a breath that is hard to find. I'm drowning in emotions that are suffocating me. My lungs are constricted, as though they won't function no matter how hard I try. I finally begin to gasp, suddenly filling my lungs with the air they were deprived of. Devin sits beside me, allowing me to collect myself as he rubs my back to calm me. I turn and throw my arms around Devin's torso, seeking warmth and comfort. He holds me tight, not saying a word. He's letting my mind and body work through the breathless torment of my nightmare.

My composure settles as my breathing returns to a normal state. "Thank you," I whisper as I pull from the warmth of his arms so I can look into his eyes.

"Stop thanking me. I'm glad I came home when I did," he says as he kisses my temple.

Devin saying he was glad he came "home" comforts me. That one little word that holds more meaning than I could possibly explain fills me with a sense of security that only he can fill. These past few days have been hell, and my house, which used to be filled with love and laughter, has not felt like home until right now in this very moment.

"What's going on in that head of yours?" Devin asks with an eyebrow arched.

"Not much. I just liked how you called this home." A shy smile touches my lips.

Devin sits quietly for a moment. I can see a multitude of expressions flash across his vibrant blue eyes. I watch as his mind works through his thoughts, as if he is trying to find his next words. I feel a little uneasy, as he never has a problem saying anything to me. Maybe my admission about him calling this home spooked him somehow.

I jump up, startling him with my unexpected movement, and head to my bathroom, closing the door behind me. I splash cold water on my face, trying to fully recover from my earlier breakdown and the fucked-up nightmare, daymare, anytimemare that seems to be on repeat in my head.

There's a soft knock on the bathroom door, followed by Devin's low voice. "Hey, Lex, are you OK?"

"I'm fine. I just need a minute."

A minute isn't long enough for me to gather myself, so I decide to take a quick shower. My body is wound tight, my stomach is in knots, and I'm hoping the hot water will help ease some of the tension coiled in my neck and shoulders. Once I've stripped down and stepped into the shower, I can't stop the tears that freely trickle from my eyes. I guess once you give in to the grieving process, it doesn't just let up because you want it to. I go from simple tears to crying to full-blown devastating sobs within minutes. My head and forearms lean against the cool shower tile as the hot water races down my back. Stabs of pain shoot through my heart as if it were being cut open from the inside out. My legs give way as I drop to my knees on the shower floor, arms wrapped tight around my torso as if I'm trying to protect myself, rocking back and forth, trying to ease away the merciless pain and desolation of losing my mom and dad. I can't do this. I can't make it in this world without their love, support, and guidance. God, I hate this. I hate every fucking second of this. I want the pain to cease.

I jump when the shower shuts off and Devin wraps a towel around my body. He helps ease me off the floor, making sure I'm covered. What is it with me and needing help getting out of my shower? We both exit from the shower, and Devin grabs my robe, wrapping it over my shoulders, coaxing my arms through the sleeves. His eyes never leave my face as he removes the towel from my torso before securing the robe tightly around my waist. He takes the towel and begins drying my soaking-wet hair. Once he has the dripping moisture removed, he hands me my comb and places a quick kiss to my forehead before turning on his heels and leaving me to finish up in the bathroom. He doesn't say a word. He simply was there to help me, again.

I quickly comb through my knotted hair and put it up in a messy bun. My reflection in the mirror reveals bloodshot eyes, dark circles, and utter sadness. I take a steadying breath before leaving my bathroom. When I emerge, I see Devin is out on the balcony, looking down the street as if he is caught in a trance. I go to my closet and dress quickly in yoga pants and a T-shirt. Right now, I only want comfort, and these clothes offer me that simple feeling.

As I walk from the closet, Devin is now leaning against the doorjamb of the French doors, staring at me with empathy. A small smile curves at his lips as he sees I'm not in meltdown mode.

"Are you OK now?" he asks warily.

I nod for fear my voice may sound otherwise.

"Can we talk?" he asks in a low, unsure tone.

I hesitate before answering, "Yes, of course we can."

"Before I begin, could you promise to hear me out and let me say my piece before you say or do anything?" His voice is shaky.

"Dev, you're scaring me."

"Just promise me, Lex, please."

"I promise," I answer as I walk over to my bed and sit down Indian-style toward the edge. My hands are fidgety, so I just clasp them together and rest them in my lap.

He rolls my desk chair over to where I'm sitting so he can sit facing me. My nerves are all over the place right now, and I don't know if I can handle Devin telling me that being here is too much for him and he needs to leave and gain space between us. His presence is keeping me somewhat sane. Losing him now would put me over the proverbial edge.

"Lex, don't look at me like you just lost your best friend. I'm not going anywhere. I just need to talk to you about a couple of things," he says as he unbinds my clutched hands and rubs his thumb over the back of the one he's kept hold of.

I let out the breath I didn't realize I was holding and physically feel my body relax a smidge with his statement. I smile at him and nod for him to continue, as I am keeping my promise not to interrupt whatever it is he needs to say to me.

Devin smiles when he sees my shoulders loosen up and then begins, "Earlier today, I went to your school to talk to the head football coach. Uh-uh, you promised," he says when he sees the look of confusion on my face and my mouth open to speak. I immediately snap it shut to keep from saying anything. He continues, "As you know, your varsity quarterback took a huge hit a couple of weekends ago, ending his high school playing days and leaving your football team with a semi-par second-string QB who can't deliver a win even if the other team forfeited. With a chance at the championship on the line, the coach is entertaining the idea of me transferring to your school and becoming the varsity QB. After I left the school, I went over to Stanford and spoke to my admissions counselor to see if transferring schools would jeopardize my football scholarship. She said that as long as I have similar college prep classes, maintain my GPA, and still play varsity football, it would not jeopardize my scholarship. She also said that attending your school will look great on my transcripts. So, my question to you is, would you like me to move in here with you so you don't have to live here alone?" Devin asks the question all while looking down at the ground, as his hands are now nervously fidgeting into knots.

It takes me a few minutes to process everything he just said to me. He wants to stay with me so I won't ever be alone. I'm in awe, shocked and speechless. My voice is but a whisper when I finally speak. "Dev, look at me, please." His eyes dart up to meet mine, and I smile as fear and uncertainty dance through his blues. "What about your parents? Have you talked to them yet?"

"I'm eighteen—an adult, just like you. Of course I'm going to talk to them, but they can't force me to stay with them. I honestly don't think they will mind as long as I stay on track and still go to Stanford."

Devin is so sure of himself and this important decision, and I know he won't do anything to screw up Stanford. This isn't just a whim for him. He's put a lot of thought into this and has already done the hardest part of the footwork. Now he or we will need to convince his parents that everything will be OK.

"Yes, Devin. It will be nice having you here. It is nice having you here. We will talk to your parents tomorrow. Sometime after meeting with the lawyer, I should be receiving my parents' ashes. Your mom and dad know this, so you should invite them to come over after they get off work."

Devin has his disarming and heart-melting megawatt smile that shows the hint of a dimple, and relief glimmers in his eyes. He leans forward, placing a soft kiss to my lips before he pulls back and sends a text from his phone. My guess is it's to his parents.

# Chapter Twelve

It's almost one o'clock by the time I leave Mr. Rocklin's office. My head is throbbing from all of the information and documents we had to go through, and my nerves are shot from the roller coaster of emotions coursing through me. I'm glad I was able to talk Devin into staying at the house instead of coming with me. I wasn't 100 percent sure when my parents' ashes were going to be delivered, and I didn't want to chance missing them.

As I slide into the driver's seat to my car and close the door, I fish out my cell phone from my purse. I had it on silent while I was with the attorney. I have a missed call from Becca and a text message from a phone number that I don't recognize. I listen to my voice mail first, making a mental note to call Becca when school is out. There is so much to tell her and Jess, and frankly, I miss them. I will need to have them over tomorrow since Devin's parents will be at the house tonight. I don't even want to think about how that conversation is going to go.

When I click on the text message, a chill runs done my spine. All it says is "MINE." My hands are shaking, as there is only one person this could possibly be from, but why not from his own cell phone? Why now? I reply back with only one word: Ethan?

I have been home about an hour and a half since I left the lawyer's office, and I never received a reply back from the unknown number. Well, if it was Ethan, I really don't have time or energy to play stupid games with him. He knows what I'm dealing with, so why would he send a chicken-shit text instead of calling me and at least admitting he made a mistake when he fucked me and took my virginity. I contemplated texting his old number to see if it was still activated, but my disappointment and hurt feelings won the internal argument I had going on in my head. I delete the message from the unknown number after looking at it for the millionth time and head out back to where Devin is sitting at the outdoor dining table, doing homework.

He looks up and smiles at me when he hears the sliding door open. I really enjoy this feeling I keep getting when he looks at me like I'm the only person in the world. It's heartwarming and comforting when I feel so used and miserable.

"Hey," he says as I take a seat across from him so I don't crowd his space where his chemistry book is open, laptop front and center and papers spread out.

"How has your morning been?" I ask.

"Busy with phone calls, homework and…" Devin hesitates for a moment before finishing, "arguing and signing for your parents' ashes."

I feel the blood drain from my face. I knew the ashes were being delivered, but now that they are here, I feel sick to my stomach. "Wait, what do you mean argue?" I ask once that part of what he had disclosed registers in my brain.

"The delivery guy was a total dick. He wasn't going to let me accept the ashes because he said you had to be the one to sign. I told him I was their nephew and you were at the lawyer's office dealing with your parents' will and your trust. After he made a phone call to the mortuary, he finally conceded to let me sign. With that being said, I put their urns in their room on the dresser. I didn't know where else to put them, and I didn't want them to be the first thing you saw when you got home."

Devin's open honesty and considerate ways are so refreshing, and the fact that he actually thought about where to put my parents' ashes makes my heart flutter with unmistakable love.

I get up from where I am sitting across from Devin and round the table, stopping in front of him. His eyes never leave mine as he turns slightly in the chair, allowing me to sit across his lap. He wraps his arms around my waist as I wrap mine around his neck, placing a gentle closed-mouth kiss on his lips. I feel his lips pull up at the corners when my lips touch his, and I know he is smiling.

"What was that for?" he asks.

"Just for being you and wonderful and amazing and to say thank you for helping with my parents' ashes."

His eyes darken with a hunger for me as he reaches up to cup my left cheek gently, bringing my face closer as his soft lips brush against mine ever so lightly, sending a rush of desire straight to my core and making my heartbeat speed up. My fingers grip the hair at the nape of his neck as I lick his lips, coaxing them to part, deepening the kiss with our tongues tangling and manipulating each other's. Devin slides an arm under the back of my knees, cradling me as he stands in one swift movement. I nuzzle into his neck as he carries me to the outside daybed and lays me down gently, resting his hard body between my thighs as he holds most of his weight off of me with one arm bent by my head. Devin's mouth is deliciously punishing mine, as if he can't get enough of me. The fingers on his free hand dig into my hip the more turned on he gets. I can feel his hardened length rubbing against my aching clit, pooling wetness in my panties. He trails kisses down my jawline and nips at my neck until he reaches my collarbone, where his tongue glides from one side to the other. A moan releases from my lips as my hands grip his firm ass, pulling him into me. Devin rocks his hips, and his own feral groan vibrates from the back of his throat.

We are so caught up in the throes of passion, and just as my hand begins descending down Devin's toned torso toward his rigid cock, we hear a throat clear. Devin instinctively jumps up, leaving me cold and flustered. We both look over at the sliding door, where George and Marie are standing with shocked expressions. I feel my face instantly heat from utter embarrassment, and I'm pretty sure I'm every shade of red at being caught in a heavy make-out session with their son.

Oh. My. God. How could we be so careless and forget that Devin's parents were coming over today? I just lie on the daybed with my arms covering my face, trying to regain my composure and dignity and slow my racing heart. If the earth opened beneath me and swallowed me whole right now, I would not complain. The next couple of hours are now going to be very uncomfortable. I know we are both legally adults, but this situation is not one I wanted to be in, ever.

George is the first to break the silence. "We knocked, and when neither of you answered, we used our spare key."

"Sorry, Dad. Obviously, we didn't hear you," Devin replies with a hint of awkwardness in his voice. I can only imagine that he is avoiding looking at either parent just as I am.

Once I finally remove my arms from over my face, I glance up at Devin, who is standing beside the daybed, his own face a shade of red. He holds his hand out to help me to my feet. I hesitantly accept it.

"Shall we go inside?" I ask everyone.

"Sure," Marie answers as she moves to start picking up Devin's mess on the table. He quickly goes over to help as a way to distract himself from the uneasiness he's probably feeling right now. This incident will make the pending conversation of Devin moving in all the more difficult when pleading his or our case. They will think we want to live together for one reason other than the true reason of me not wanting to be alone in this house that is now mine.

We have all congregated in the family room. No one is in a rush to speak first. I think Devin and I made a deliberate decision not to sit directly next to each other since we have a full cushion separating us. His parents noticed but have yet to say anything, thank God.

"So, Lexi, how did your meeting go with Mr. Rocklin today?" George asks, again in effort to break the deafening silence that is weighing heavy in the open and airy room.

Finding my voice, I begin, "It went well. There was a lot to go over, take in, and absorb when my mind just wanted to shut down. Mr. Rocklin was extremely patient with me and very thorough. Then again, Mom and Dad were very thorough. Let's just say, I will never want for anything. Between my trust fund and their absurd life insurance policies, the house and all the cars will be paid off within the month, and the sale of Lang—" A sob catches in my throat before I can finish my sentence. Devin's kneejerk reaction is to scoot toward me and gather me into his familiar embrace, offering me comfort. I know I would rather be dirt poor living in a cardboard box if it meant having my parents back in my life.

"Well, we knew they would take care of you, Alexa," Marie chimes in with a sympathetic smile. "You were their pride and joy, and they were so very proud of you." Sincerity and love are evident in her tone.

Stray tears slide down my cheeks as I continue, "Apparently, Mr. Rocklin had instructions that if something were to happen to both of them at the same time, he was to reach out to the COO and CFO of Langley to offer up the sale of my mom's business, since both Mom and Dad knew that I wouldn't be following in Mom's footsteps. With that being said, I have accepted their extremely generous offer, which was faxed over before my arrival this morning. I was also given a key to a safe deposit box, but I was too overwhelmed when I left Mr. Rocklin's office, so I didn't bother to stop on my way home."

"Are we still set on having the party celebrating your parents' lives this Saturday, or did you want to postpone?" George asks.

Marie speaks before I have a chance to answer George. "Lexi, if you want to postpone, it's alright to do so. I can reschedule the caterer, party rental company, and florist and send out an e-mail to all who are invited. It really is not a problem if you aren't ready."

"No, it really is fine. Everything is already in place, and I think the sooner I do this, the sooner I can move forward, go through my stages of grieving, concentrate fully on school, and graduate in a few months."

Letting out a slight sigh of relief, George replies, "Well, OK, then. It's settled. A big bash for your parents will go on as planned this Saturday."

Since I'm still sitting against Devin's side, I feel his body tense. I'm sure he is trying to find the best way to bring up moving in with me, but how do you bring up something like that after being interrupted in our compromising position earlier? Damn us for not being more careful.

"What's on your mind, Son?" George asks Devin. I'm sure he can see the cogs turning in his son's head, as the furrowed expression on his face gives away he is deep in thought.

"Huh?" Devin replies as he is pulled back into the conversation.

"You look like you want to say something, so I asked what's on your mind." George looks to Devin with a raised eyebrow.

Devin smiles at his parents and asks them not to interrupt until he's finished with what he wants to say. Both agreed skeptically, and Devin waited a few moments to gather his composure before he proceeded to explain to them everything he had to me earlier, except with them he added in that he was an adult now and could make this decision with or without their blessing. He was hoping it would be with their blessing since he is very close with his parents.

George and Marie sit in silence, staring at the two of us. I am relieved to see that shock isn't the expression plastered on their faces, but it is hard to gauge what they are feeling or even thinking. It looks more like uncertainty. Uncertainty of what to say or how to handle the bomb their son just dropped on them. Devin reaches over and entwines his fingers with mine. He begins rubbing the back of my hand fervently with his thumb. I'm sure he did this to help with his nerves. Lord knows my hands were shaking.

Marie looks down at our hands clasped together, and a hint of a smile creeps up across her lips. George, on the other hand, has a frown.

"Ugh! The silence is killing me," Devin says, slightly agitated. "One of you please say something? Yell, don't yell, but for the love of God, speak, please. Don't just sit there and stare at us like we've grown second heads."

Marie laughs out loud at her son's frustration. George's lips finally quirk into a grin.

"Son, we had a feeling this conversation was going to come up. For one thing, your coach called me today to see if I knew what you were up to, so it gave your mother and me a chance to discuss this before we came over," George says, finally speaking. Amusement dances in his eyes as he watches Devin squirm in his seat.

I can't help the smile that spreads across my face. Huh, they already knew.

"You both are adults, and you both have been raised with values and morals. Your heads are on straight, and we believe that Lexi needs you here, Dev. This is going to be hard for her," Marie says as she smiles at me briefly, "and we hope that you can be the man she needs to help her through this trying time. We're proud of you, Devin," she says with adoration and love for her son.

Devin lets out a sigh of relief. "Why didn't you guys just say something instead of making me, or us, sit here and squirm in our seats?"

"Hell, Son, that was funny to watch. Plus, we wanted to see if you would step up and be an adult about it by bringing up the topic yourself," George replies.

Everyone laughs as the tension leaves the family room.

"I know the timing to bring this up is not ideal, and I should have asked earlier, but, Lexi, honey, did you get the urns today?" Marie asks.

"Yeah, they are in my parents' bedroom where Devin put them. I haven't seen them yet," I answer with fresh tears pooling in my eyes. Devin's hand grips mine a little tighter, letting me know he's here for me. He leans over and places a kiss to my temple before standing.

"I'll go grab them if you want, Lex," Devin says.

"OK." It's all I can squeak out.

Devin walks out of the family room and quickly returns with my parents' ashes. He sets the urns on the coffee table in front of me. My stomach is in knots, and I feel light-headed. Tears stream freely as I stare at the table.

My dad's urn is gun-metal gray with a Chinese-style dragon etched on one side of the metal urn and the American flag with a bald eagle in flight etched on the opposite side. It's a very manly urn. I had the dragon added since my dad had a few tattoos that were similar in style, and I wanted the urn to be uniquely his. Mom's urn is delicate and feminine, just like she was. Her urn is white with full-bloom cherry blossom trees circling it, and the lid houses a cushion-cut emerald embedded in the center. Cherry blossom trees were her favorite, and she loved that time of year when they bloomed. The emerald reminded me of her eyes, which shone with so much love.

"Wow, Lexi. Those are beautiful," Marie says with tears running down her face now.

"Thank you."

I welcome this silence between us all. It's a moment of mourning that we are sharing, and it feels right.

"Well, you two, we have to hit the road. As always, early day tomorrow," George says as he stands, reaching down to help Marie to her feet. When I glance up, I can see his eyes are red. George is a strong man, and to see his emotions getting the best of him in this moment fills my heart with so much love for him. This is my only family now, and I love them dearly.

Devin and I walk his parents to the door and say our good-byes. George agrees to help Devin move the following weekend, since the upcoming weekend is the remembrance party.

"Love you, guys," Devin says.

"Love you too, Son," his dad says before Devin shuts the door.

# Chapter Thirteen

Well, that went better than I thought it would. I feel a huge weight lifted off of my shoulders. I also don't have the dreaded feeling of loneliness in my gut now that Devin will be living here with me. I'm not sure how we will handle this once he has officially moved in, but right now, that is not what I want to think about.

"Hey, Dev?" I say in a louder-than-normal voice, since I don't know where he's gone.

"Yeah," he answers, coming out of my parents' bedroom and closing the doors behind him.

"What are you doing in there?"

"I was just putting the urns back on the dresser until you are ready for them to be out and have decided where you want them displayed," he answers cautiously. I can hear the hesitation in his voice, as if he didn't know if he should have moved them again.

"Thank you," I reply, offering him a smile. I see the tension around his eyes ease immediately. "It's been a long, emotional day, and I'm exhausted. I'm going to go to bed," I tell him as I head upstairs to my bedroom.

"OK. I'm going to do some more homework and watch some TV."

"Good night, Dev."

"Night, Lex."

I'm not sure how long I've been asleep, but I wake up when I feel an arm circle around my waist and a featherlight kiss brush across my bare shoulder.

I turn my head slightly to look over my shoulder and see Devin is just coming to bed. He is snuggling up against my back.

"I'm sorry. I didn't mean to wake you," he says quietly. The heat of his breath on the back of my neck sends goose bumps down my spine. I roll over so I'm lying on my back, keeping my head turned so I can see his strikingly handsome face, which is barely visible by the moonlight shining through my French doors to the balcony.

"God, you're beautiful," Devin says, staring deep into my soul as he brushes the back of his knuckles down my cheek. My stomach does a flip and my sex clenches at the intimate touch of his hand. "You have the face of an angel and the most stunning brown eyes with a glint of gold that twinkles when you are happy or aroused." He gives me a smirk, as I'm sure my eyes are definitely giving away how his touch and his words are affecting me. "And these sexy-as-sin curves drive me wild," he says as his hand slides slowly down my side to my hip and then back up again. "Hell, they probably drive every man wild, but right now, they belong to me. But, Lexi, what separates you from every other woman, what makes you unique and special, is this right here." Devin leans in and places a kiss above my left breast where my heart is slamming against my chest from the intimacy of this conversation. My breath hitches as his lips leave my heated skin.

I rotate to my side so we are face-to-face and lean forward just enough to place a kiss on his full lips. His left hand trails back down my side and rests at my hip, and he pulls me closer, licking my lips, silently asking for permission to enter my mouth. My lips part as I oblige willingly. Devin's kisses are tender and sweet. He tastes of minty toothpaste, as if he had just brushed his teeth before coming to bed. He draws my bottom lip between his teeth before his tongue darts back into my mouth. He's moved me so I am now lying on my back again, and he situates himself between my thighs. All that separates us are my boy shorts and camisole and his boxer briefs.

His hand slides under the hem of my camisole and up my torso to find my bare breast. My nipples react instantly to his touch as he gently kneads my breasts with his free hand, teasing my tight bud between his forefinger and thumb. My back arches, pushing my breast harder into his hand. I can feel his erection straining against his boxer briefs as he is pressing against my clit. A moan slips from my lips. His mouth is sucking lightly on my neck as I rock my hips against his thick length, trying to get some friction to help with the building pressure in my core.

I slide my hand down his washboard abs, over the sexy V, and between his heated skin and boxers. I gently grip his steel length, my fingertips barely touching as I start to stroke his silky hardness. He growls and bites down on the sensitive spot at the crook of my neck as he moves his hips, assisting me with the first hand job I've ever given.

Devin sits back on his haunches, quickly pulling me up with him, his hands pulling my camisole over my head. He hisses a sigh of pleasure as he stares at my heavy-with-desire breasts before his mouth crushes back into mine, bruising my already swollen lips as he lays me back down.

He pulls back just enough to make me whimper at the loss of our connection. Devin looks into my eyes as if he is asking for permission to continue. I drag my bottom lip between my teeth before I reach down and wiggle out of my boy shorts. Once I have kicked them off, I slide my hands over his hips, tugging down his boxer briefs, springing his erection free from confinement. I feel the inferno burning deep in my core and the wetness between my legs. The anticipation is killing me, and I don't know how much longer I can hold out before I actually start begging. I've been wound up since our afternoon make out session outside. All I want is for Devin to be inside me, to feel a deeper connection to him.

Devin leans forward, taking my mouth gently this time. Our tongues glide languidly over each other's. His hand slides down my stomach, over my pubic bone, and brushes ever so lightly across my sensitive nub before wetting his finger with my arousal and sliding it between my slick folds. My sex instantly tightens around his digit as I moan with pleasure.

"Fuck, Lex. You feel amazing." Devin's voice is gruff and deep.

"Make love to me, Dev. I need you inside me. Please," I beg with my barely audible voice.

"Hang on, baby. I want to enjoy feeling you like this first," he says as he slips a second finger inside me, his palm rubbing against my clit. My body reacts with trembles as I feel him working his fingers in and out of my dripping-wet pussy. He adjusts his hand, crooking his fingers just enough to hit that pleasure spot on the front of my velvety wall as he rubs my clit in a circular motion, adding pressure with his thumb. This sends me spiraling over the edge. My sex tightens around his fingers as I feel the heated rush of my orgasm surge through me. Devin's name escapes through panted breaths as I hurtle into my very own erotic oblivion. My heart is racing, my breaths are heavy, and my body is shaking as it tries to recover from the pleasure Devin selflessly gave me. I open my eyes to see Devin smiling down at me with desire burning dark in his blue eyes.

"Watching you come was the hottest thing I have ever seen," he whispers in my ear and then places a kiss right below it.

His words make me blush with embarrassment, and I'm thankful it's dark enough in my room that he can't witness it. Devin moves to cover my body with his. He begins to work his hips, rubbing against my slick folds to coat his cock with my postorgasmic juices. I can feel the thick head of his erection pressing against my entrance as he gently pushes forward. I relax a bit so I can allow him to enter me. I can feel Devin is only partially inside me when he pulls back, leaving just the tip in before thrusting forward one last time, stretching me, filling me completely as I take all of him. He groans as he stills, allowing me to adjust to the fullness.

"Oh God, Devin," I moan as my quivering sex adjusts and tightens around his invasion.

"You feel so fucking good, Alexa," he murmurs as he begins to move his hips gently back and forth. I can already feel my core tightening again, wanting the release. Devin hasn't even begun to work me, but my greedy sex is hypersensitive as his cock hits all the right nerves within my velvety walls.

"I need you to go faster, Dev," I beg.

"I won't last if I do, Lex. Your warmth and tightness is making it hard for me to hang in there."

"Believe me, baby, I'm almost there. Please, I need you to go harder and faster." Begging is not beneath me in this moment of need.

With my words, Devin's mouth claims mine as he begins pumping harder and faster into me, my hips meeting his with every thrust. Our bodies easily glide against each other with sweat glistening. I can feel him grow bigger inside me as my sex grips around his steel shaft. He's close, and with that thought, I tumble back into my own erotic oblivion again.

"Devin!" I yell as my orgasm crashes through me like a bull plowing through a China shop. He thrusts two more times before I feel his heated release spurt deep inside me. A guttural growl mixed with my name erupts from his throat as his body convulses, and my greedy pussy milks every last drop from him.

Devin rolls off of me so he doesn't smother me with the weight of his body, and he lies next to me with a hand splayed across my abdomen. We are both breathing heavily, coming down from our passionate lovemaking. I roll to my side so I can see Devin's face. His head turns so his eyes meet mine.

"That was incredible, Dev," I say with a shaky breath.

"Not too bad for my first time, then?" he asks shyly.

"Wait. What? You were a virgin?"

"Well, yeah. I mean I've had hand jobs and blow jobs, but I've never gone down on a girl or done the deed," he admits. "As much as I sound like a sappy chick right now, it never felt right because they weren't you, Lexi."

I smile at the thought that I'm Devin's first. He should have been my first, but I gave that gift to Ethan. God, I am so stupid.

I put my finger to his lips to keep him from continuing. "I don't need to know what you have done with other girls. Please spare me the details," I say with a giggle.

"Alexa," he says in a whisper.

"Yeah, Dev?"

"I love you."

My heart feels like it's going to burst with the all the feelings I have for Devin. I never in my life thought we would be here, right now, in this moment. I can't help but think my parents brought him back to me, knowing I would need his strength and love. Tears fill my eyes, but for the first time in days, these tears are happy.

I smile at Devin, placing a kiss on his puffy lips, and whisper back, "I love you too."

$\backsim_\circledcirc$

I wake up to Devin's morning hard-on pressed against my leg, and he's lazily drawing circles with his finger around my belly button.

"Good morning, gorgeous," he says with freshly brushed teeth and heated desire already gleaming in his eyes.

I immediately cover my mouth, since I wasn't so lucky to wake first and brush my teeth, when I tease, "You're insatiable." My libido is fully awake, and my nub is already throbbing and needy, wanting Devin's fingers to move below my belly button.

Devin leans in to kiss me, but I jump out of bed and run across the room to the bathroom, shutting the door. I can hear him laughing at me. Yelling from the bathroom, I tell Devin, "Sorry, but I have to take care of morning breath and other business."

"Lex, if it means seeing your naked sexiness run across the room again, I don't care what you have to do in there," he jokes back from the other room.

I completely forgot that I was naked when I decided to dart across the bedroom. Thankful for a little privacy, I'm glad Devin can't see the blush that heats my cheeks from his teasing comment. I hurry to take care of my morning needs when I hear Devin call from the bedroom that someone is knocking at the front door. "Do you want me to answer it?" he asks.

"No, I will be right out. I don't want you moving from that bed, because we have some unfinished business to take care of." I hear his throaty laugh, and it brings a stupid grin to my face. Being with Devin is easy, and it feels right. Ethan was always hot but complicated.

I grab my robe, securing it around my body, and exit the bathroom. Devin is lying propped up by pillows on the bed with the sheet strategically placed just below the V that leads down to his extraordinary cock. I can see the distinctive outline of his erection, and I immediately lick my lips as wetness pools between my thighs. I'm surprised I don't have to wipe drool from the corner of my mouth since Devin is most definitely drool worthy and sexy as hell.

"Lex, as much as I'm enjoying that look on your face right now, you have to get the door, remember?" He laughs again, bringing my attention back to his face.

"Yeah, r-right," I stutter, since I'm now sexually flustered. I head down to the front door when I hear the doorbell ring. I unlock the deadbolt and open the door, surprised to see Olivia Gage standing there.

"Alexa, did I catch you at a bad time?" she asks with one of her perfectly manicured eyebrows arched and her eyes skimming over my disheveled appearance. The coldness of her stare makes me uneasy.

"Um, no. Not at all. What can I do for you, Olivia?" I ask. Olivia hasn't been over to my house since we first moved in, so I'm curious as to why she's here all of a sudden.

"Have you heard from my son, Lexi?" she asks with an unsettling tone to her voice and something like disgust in her eyes.

What the fuck?

"No, I haven't heard from Ethan since he left. Is something wrong? Is he OK?" I can't help the worry that suddenly takes over my emotions. As much as I feel like I've been used by Ethan, I still wouldn't want something bad to happen to him.

"Nothing is wrong. Ethan is fine. I was just curious if he has tried to contact you in any way."

OK, this conversation is awkward and weird, and I don't like the direction it is heading. A shiver runs down my spine, and coldness trickles through my veins.

"Well, I don't see how it's any of your business, but he hasn't, so if you will excuse me, I have a long day ahead of me," I snap back defensively.

The woman makes me feel I have to defend myself to her.

"He is my son, and he is my business. He doesn't love you, Alexa. He will never love you," she chides.

Where in the hell is this coming from? She is seriously giving me the creeps now. "Look, Olivia, this conversation is making me uncomfortable, and I'm not exactly sure what you are getting at, but I really do need to get ready for my day, so if that will be all, I hope you have a fantastic day." The last part drips with sarcasm as I close the door in her face.

I go back to my room, where Devin is exactly how I left him. My recent conversation with Olivia has not had any negative influence on my libido once my eyes take in Devin's handsome face with his slightly curved nose from being broken when we were kids; golden, chiseled chest; sculpted abs; and that mouthwatering fucking V. Yummy.

"Who was at the door?" he asks, eyeing me suspiciously.

"Olivia, Ethan's mom. Look, I don't want her to ruin our morning or our day, so let's not talk about her," I answer as I untie my robe, letting it slide down my shoulders and off my body to pool at my feet, hoping it will distract Devin. Lucky for me, it does. Devin sucks in a breath as his eyes wander shamelessly over my body, devouring me with each pass. He licks his lips as if he can't wait to taste me.

"I am the luckiest guy in the world to have the sexiest woman ever crawling back into bed to make love to me," he says as I slide in under the sheet next to him. Devin turns just enough to cup my face, bringing his lips to mine for a sweet closed-mouth kiss. "God, I've waited all morning just for that one little kiss," he says with a boyish grin.

"Devin, I have no clue what I'm doing since I'm not experienced, but ever since I've seen you lying here naked this morning with your, you know…" I blush as my eyes travel down the length of his torso and stop at the very present sheeted outline of his steel manliness. "I have wanted to run my tongue down your amazing body and have your, uh, penis in my mouth." My face is blazing hot right now as embarrassment consumes me. Devin hasn't said or done anything to make me feel embarrassed of my words, but I can't help the sudden shyness. He said he's had blow jobs before, and since I have never given one, I'm afraid I will be horrible and he won't enjoy it.

"Babe, I want nothing more right now than to have your luscious lips wrapped around my cock," he replies.

"But what if—"

Devin stops me with a passionate kiss, his tongue dominating, owning my mouth. My arousal drips from my folds just from this simple form of affection. I pull back and try again. "Dev—" His hand thrusts into my hair at the back of my neck, his mouth possessing mine again before I can finish the sentence.

After a few dizzying minutes have passed, Devin says, "We're both new at this, Lex. That is what makes this all the more special and fun. We get to learn and experiment together. I have no clue what I'm doing, but I know for damn sure I want to explore your body. I want to know what makes you feel good, what makes you moan that sweet sound when you're ready to come. I want to find every erogenous zone on your body that makes the gold in your eyes twinkle. I want to worship and love you, Lex. That's all I've ever wanted."

Devin's words are empowering and give me the confidence that I need, because I want all the same things. I want to explore every inch of him. I want to make him feel cherished and loved. I want to be his pleasure and sexual release.

A seductive smile creeps across my lips. My eyelids are heavy with want, my core feels like liquid lava as desire hits me, and my clit yearns for stimulation. I gradually begin trailing kisses mixed with flicks of my tongue down Devin's chest. My slick sex is rubbing against Devin's leg, which I am straddling as I descend. This position is alleviating some of my needed stimulation but not enough to release the built-up pressure. An animalistic groan reverberates from his chest when I pass over both of the flat discs of his nipples, nipping each one with equal attentiveness as my nails drag down the length of his flexed abs. I continue my descent, licking around his belly button, followed by kisses down his groomed happy trail before tracing my tongue from one side of his sexy-as-hell V to the other. His hands fist in my hair just at my scalp as I get closer to his bobbing cock.

After settling myself between his legs, I glance up to see if I'm affecting Devin as he does me. I can't help the hint of a smile of satisfaction that forms on my mouth as I see undeniable lust, passion, and love staring down at me through hooded blue eyes. Fueled by his appreciation, I am quick to remember certain scenes in the pornos my mom gave me to watch as a learning tool. I wrap one hand around the base of Devin's thick shaft, keeping the other hand just to the outside of his thigh for upper body support as I lick my lips in preparation to take his mushroom head dripping with precome into my mouth. A jagged hiss escapes his lips as I circle my tongue around the ridge, tasting the translucent salty goodness, before taking him deep into my mouth. The tip of his head hits the back of my throat before my lips even reach the hand gripping the base of his cock. I want to take more, but Devin's body shudders just as I sink my warm, wet mouth down as far as I can go. I hollow my cheeks as I come back up, adding pressure from my tongue to the underside of Devin's rigid perfection. I repeat the motion again and again as my hand follows my mouth to the tip and then back down again to the base. Devin's hips begin to thrust, meeting my rhythm, breathing wanton, eyes closed, hands fisted in my hair. I can only hope Devin is lost in the ecstasy of pleasure my mouth is providing. I keep the pace steady when, out of nowhere, Devin shifts quickly, pulling my body up the length of his, punishing my already plump lips with a kiss so heady and frenzied.

I pull back. Concern clearly etched on my face. "Did I hurt you? Did I do something wrong? Was I that bad?" The words are flying out of my mouth in succession as my paranoia of inexperience sets in.

"God, no! That felt fucking amazing! I was going to come, and we haven't even begun yet." Devin's answer relieves my anxiety. "If I didn't know any better, I would have thought you've done that before, a few times."

"Dev, you will be honest with me if something I do doesn't feel good, right? Actually, I need you to be honest with me," I ask hesitantly, not sure if I would really want to know that I'm not doing something right or that something doesn't feel good, but the perfectionist in me wants to please, needs to please.

"Baby, I promise, as long as you do the same for me," he says sweetly.

"I promise, Dev." I think I just fell more in love with my best friend, if that is even possible.

We spend the rest of the morning making love in my bed, the shower, and back in my bed again before we set out separately for our day. After all of that sex, you would think I would be completely sated, but I still want more of Devin. I don't think I will ever get enough of him.

# Chapter Fourteen

Devin is out trying to get his school transfer taken care of while I finally muster the courage to head to the bank where the safe deposit box is located. After I check in with the lady at the counter, she smiles and asks me to have a seat to wait for the bank manager. I'm not sure if there's an issue or if this is protocol, so I turn to take my seat in the waiting area. Roughly ten minutes pass before a tall man with a lean build, wearing a perfectly fitted three-piece navy-blue pinstriped suit, begins to walk toward me. His salt-and-pepper hair is cut short, and the stern expression on his face gives him that "all business, no play" look.

"Alexa Morgan, I'm David Burge, the bank manager," he says in a sophisticated tone as his hand reaches out to shake mine.

"Nice to meet you, Mr. Burge," I greet him with a solid handshake once I'm on my feet.

"We are very sorry to hear about Joseph and Jeanine." His eyes reflect sympathy. "Your parents have been patrons of my bank for a very long time, and I do hope you will continue to bank with us," he says, offering a smile.

Ah, that's his game. He doesn't want to lose my business because that would be a lot of money his bank would lose. "I don't see a reason I wouldn't," I admit.

"Well, I'm very glad to hear that, Ms. Morgan. So Anna tells me you're here to gain access to your safe deposit box. Please follow me."

I follow Mr. Burge across the marble floor toward an elevator that is accessed with a badge and a PIN code. Once we have entered, Mr. Burge presses a button, and the elevator descends downward one level. When the doors open, I am immediately in awe of my surroundings. The rich cherrywood wainscoting lines each of the walls, stretching all the way down the corridor. There are several doors that line the hallway toward a vault-style door at the end. Modern art paintings hang between each of the doors, adding a splash of color to the ornate space. To the left of the elevator is a large mahogany desk with a security guard sitting behind it, looking at his monitors.

"Bob, this is Alexa Morgan. Please escort her to safe deposit box ten fifteen and show her to one of the private rooms," Mr. Burge instructs the security guard before turning back to the elevator and leaving me in the hands of the security guard.

The box number was not lost on me, since it's the month and day of my birth. Only my parents would do something like that. It actually makes me smile. They were thorough.

Once we retrieve the safe deposit box, Bob, the security guard, leaves me in my private room, which looks the same as the vault lobby but the room has a small mahogany table with four chairs around it instead of a desk. I choose to sit in the chair facing the door. I'm not sure why, but having my back to the closed door in such a confined space with no windows kind of freaks me out.

I slowly open the box, as if a snake were going to spring out and bite me. I laugh at myself for being silly. Once I have the box fully open, I see a few stacks of bundled money—thirty thousand dollars, to be exact. Next to the money are two envelopes addressed to me. One envelope has my dad's all-capitalized engineer-style writing, and the other has my mom's perfect cursive penmanship. All of a sudden, the air is sucked out of the tiny room, and my head is spinning. I feel dizzy and lightheaded. I'm not sure what I expected to find here, but seeing envelopes addressed to me from Mom and Dad was not on the list.

My forehead is resting on the cool top of the table as I try to even out my breathing. I need to get a grip. Hyperventilating is not an option right now. Once I have calmed down a bit, I stand, walk over to the door, and open it. I ask Bob if I can get some water, if it isn't too much trouble. He nods, and I close the door again before going back to where I was sitting. A few minutes pass, and Bob knocks, waiting for me to answer. I tell him to enter, and he places a chilled bottle of water and a box of Kleenex on the table in front of me.

"Thank you, Bob," I say in appreciation for both items he brought me.

"It's not a problem, Lexi. Your mom and dad were great people. I will miss them dearly." His genuine smile reaches his kind eyes.

"You know my nickname. How is that? Oh, so you know them?"

"Yes, I do. More so I knew your dad, Joseph. He was the one who was always here, and I've known him prior to his marriage to Jeanine. We used to bowl together back in the day before his job became so demanding and secretive."

That little bit of information Bob just gave me makes me feel better for some reason. "Thank you again for accommodating me. This isn't easy for me." I smile pathetically at the old man.

"Take your time, Lexi. There isn't a time limit on how long you can be in here. If you need anything, please don't hesitate to ask. Your dad would want you to be taken care of."

Bob turns, leaving me with my box and its contents. I stare blankly at both envelopes, wondering if I should take them and read them in the comfort and privacy of my own home or if I should get it over with and read them here in the confines of this small room. I choose home. The longer I sit here, the more it feels like the room is closing in. Besides, whatever these letters have written on them, I will need Devin's strong arms comforting me as I fall to pieces. I take the letters and put them in my purse. I glance down at the money, but right now, I don't need it, so I just leave all of it in the box. After closing the lid, I head out to Bob so we can put the safety deposit box away.

"It was a pleasure finally meeting you, Lexi," Bob says as he swipes his access card and enters his PIN for the elevator. "I'm sorry it was under these circumstances." He smiles again with kindness dancing in his eyes.

"Yes, it was, Bob," I say as I shake his hand. The elevator dings as the doors open. I step inside, and Bob presses the button to take me back to the main floor of the bank. Within seconds, I am stepping out of the elevator and heading toward the exit of the bank when Mr. Burge steps in front of me, stopping me in my tracks.

"I hope everything was satisfactory, Ms. Morgan?" Mr. Burge asks.

"I guess so," I reply, not quite sure how to answer that question. Why wouldn't it be?

"Very well. We hope to see you soon, then," he says and then turns on his heels and stalks off toward the elevator I just exited.

The day is gloomy with Bay Area overcast, so I decide on trying to relax in the family room with the television on low as I do a few more of my school assignments. My mind isn't on the work, since the two envelopes are staring at me from the coffee table. I'm struggling to wait until Devin gets home before opening them, but the task is becoming more difficult. The clock on my laptop says it's four fifteen, so I decide to text Devin to see what time he plans to be home.

Me: Hey. What's your ETA?

Devin: Sorry babe. I'm still in Fremont. I figured I would hang with some of the guys from the team before I head back.
Me: Ok.
Devin: Are you ok? Do you need me to come home now?
Me: I'm fine. I was just checking in.
I feel horrible for lying to Devin, knowing damn well I'm not fine, but I don't want to be the needy girl. He deserves and needs to hang out with his friends, especially since he won't get to see them as often now that he will be living here and attending my high school going forward.
Devin: I will be home around 8 or so.
Me: K. XO
Devin: Love u

Now what the hell am I going to do? I can't focus on school, and these letters are driving me crazy just sitting there on the table. I consider texting the twins, but I'm not in the mood to explain everything that has happened since the earthquake just yet. I'm saving that conversation for after the party on Saturday. I want to tell them everything and think for a second that maybe laying everything out there will help with my grieving, but those damn letters keep me from texting Jessa and Becca.

I finally give up on homework, close my laptop in frustration, and toss it on the cushion beside me. I get up and cross over to the bar. I grab the Jack Daniel's bottle and a tumbler and pour myself a hefty drink. Shots are not going to help me right now.

I snatch the envelopes off the coffee table and head out to the second garage. Once inside, I feel a sense of calm. It's almost as if my dad's arms are wrapped around me. We spent a lot of quality father-daughter time out here, so I guess that would make sense.

The body of the AC Shelby Cobra is lying next to the frame, and the

427 motor is dangling from the engine hoist, waiting to be installed. Seeing the car almost complete makes me want to finish it that much sooner so I can drive it. I take a drink from my glass, welcoming the burn as it slides down the back of my throat.

I walk over to the car and sit down in the passenger-side bucket seat. Neither of the seats are bolted down yet, but Dad and I needed a little more room to maneuver around the car when we worked on it, so we placed them in the car. Taking another swig of the whiskey, I look down in my lap at the beckoning envelopes. Not being able to wait any longer, I set the tumbler on the floorboard and pick up the letter from my mom first, putting Dad's on the driver's seat. With shaky hands, I tear into it and begin reading.

*My Dearest Lexi,*

*If you are reading this letter, that means something has happened to me or to us and I am no longer in your life. Writing this does not come easy, and it kills me that I am writing such a letter, but your father insisted it be done. We never wanted you to have any doubts about our love for you.*

*There are so many defining moments that I'm afraid I will miss in your lifetime, but never for one second think that I wouldn't trade my soul to the devil to be with you still. I cherish our time together as mother and daughter, and I know with every fiber of my heart that you did as well. Your dad is such an amazing man, and the day that I met him was the day I was given the greatest gift in the world—you.*

*I do not want you to be sad. I want you to hold your head high, square your shoulders, and be proud of who you are. Live life to the fullest and take nothing for granted. Be happy, Alexa. Reach for the stars and accomplish everything you set out to do. Never let anyone tell you that you can't do something, because I know in my heart that you will succeed once you set your mind to it. You are your father's daughter, after all. Just like I know you got into Stanford even if the acceptance letter hasn't come yet. You wanted it, you worked hard for it, and Stanford will be yours without a doubt.*

*I am so very proud of the young lady you have blossomed into over the years. Never forget that, Lexi. You are my daughter, my world, and all I ever want for you is to be truly happy.*

*I love you, Lexi, forever and always.*

*Love, Mom*

The uncontrollable sobbing that torments my body has crocodile droplets of tears dripping onto the letter my mom wrote to me. I wipe it against my jeans, hoping I don't ruin the sweetest letter ever. My chest is tight as the pain splinters through my broken heart. I fold the slightly smeared letter back into the envelope and place it on the driver's seat next to me.

I chug the rest of the Jack and go back to the house to pour myself another. If Mom's letter is doing this to me, I can only imagine what my dad's is going to do.

Once I've refilled my tumbler and taken a large gulp, I head back to the garage. I sit back down in the car, reaching over to grab the envelope from my dad. I take one more drink of the amber liquid before setting it on the floorboard like last time and tear into the envelope. I hadn't noticed the bulkiness to the envelope earlier, but once I have it open, a small key on a chain falls into my lap. Hmmm?

*My Princess,*

*Knowing that you are reading this means I or we are no longer alive, and my heart is breaking as I write my final good-bye to my beautiful daughter.*

*There are no words to express how proud I am of you and how happy you have made my life. Even through your stubborn streaks, you were and always will be my pride and joy. The one thing in this life I didn't mess up.*

*I know you are probably falling apart right now because you have a heart as big as the galaxy, but you are strong and will get through this. Never be afraid to ask for help or to lean on those still in your life when you need them most. Most importantly, never be afraid to go after what you want in life. Just knock and doors will open wide for you.*

*Be happy, my princess, because that is all I ever wanted for you. With that being said, the money in the safe deposit box is to finish our project. Enjoy the car, Alexa. Let her help heal the pain and emptiness you are feeling. Whenever you're behind the wheel, know I am right there with you. My blood courses through your veins so I have no doubts that you won't be able to drive her without smiling and feeling alive as the wind whips through your hair and the rumble of her engine vibrates your entire body. I'm saying it again—enjoy her for me, for us.*

*Once last thing: the key enclosed opens a floor safe under the carpet in your mom's closet in the far right corner. Open the safe now. Do not wait.*

*I love you, princess, more than anything. Never, ever forget that.*

*Love Always, Daddy*

*P.S. As hard as it will be for you to do, shred the letters, including your mom's.*

These letters were written recently—well, at least since I sent in my college applications. It's almost as if my parents knew they both would not be here anymore. Eerie chills run down my spine. There was no way to know about the earthquake that would cause the accident that took their lives. Why does this feel off, all of sudden?

The tears I was crying as I read my dad's heartfelt good-bye cease as I reread the paragraph about the key. In this moment, both fear and curiosity take precedence over my grieving. I down the last of my drink, grab the letters and the key, and head to my parents' bedroom. I sway as I stand. The two stiff drinks I have consumed have hit me hard. Damn me for drinking on an empty stomach, again. Ethan would have my ass if he saw me right now.

Whoa, where did that thought come from? I couldn't care less what Ethan would or would not do to my drunken ass. I don't even know why he popped into my head.

Shaking off the fuzzy feeling, I close up the garage and head into the house. Once I have entered the master bedroom, the air leaves my lungs when I see the urns perched on the dresser. When will this get easier? The small key digs into the palm of my tightly clutched hand, reminding me why I have come in here. I take a deep breath and cross to my mom's closet. I immediately drop to my knees and move aside her designer shoeboxes that are stacked in the far-right corner. I pull up the carpet from the corner, revealing a small floor safe, just as my dad said. I insert the key to open the safe, and it does so with ease. Inside, there is a single envelope, again with my name on it. Like the other two letters, I tear into it and begin reading.

*Alexa,*

*This is very important and highly confidential. I have no right to put this on you, but I had no other option and absolutely no one else I can trust, not even George and Marie. At this time, no one should come for the contents on the below taped micro-SD card, but if a man by the name of Viper happens to show up looking for the memory card, give it to him but no one else, especially anyone from my work. I know you are wondering how you will know who Viper is. You won't be able to mistake the man who stands taller than six foot, very muscular with military looks, and speaks with an English accent. Also, he has a viper tattooed on the back of his left hand.*

*Princess, this is important. Do not look at the documents on the memory card. Your safety and life depend on your "lack" of knowledge. Hide the micro-SD but do not hide it at the bank. I have all faith in you that you will keep this information safe and out of corrupt hands.*

*Again, I'm sorry to leave this burden with you, but I had no choice. Remember to shred all three letters now. Follow my instructions exactly as I explained, and you will be safe. I promise.*

*I love you, princess.*

I am scared and shaking. I wish Devin was here, but I'm glad he isn't. I wouldn't want this new burden put onto his shoulders too. Besides, Dad said no one is to know about this, and he trusted only me. I detach the micro-SD, examine it, and out of curiosity, I immediately want to grab my laptop from the couch and open the file, but my dad trusted me to keep it safe and not view the contents. I remember seeing a piece of carpet sticking up by the seat track in the Cobra, which I will mount the bucket seat to. Before I head back to the garage, I read all three letters one last time. These will forever be the last words I receive from my parents. Not wanting to do it but surrendering to do as my father had asked, I shred the letters. Afterward, I traipse back to the Cobra for the third time this afternoon.

I run back outside, open the door, and kneel down on the passenger side of the car. I pull back the piece of carpet just enough, and I can tell that this memory card will fit perfectly and will never be detected through the thick carpet covering. I grab tape to help keep it in place.

Once I have taped it to the metal frame, I tuck the carpet back under the track. As a bead of sweat forms above my upper lip, I think to myself that I really hope no one knows I have it or finds it here.

I close up the garage again and run back to the house and into my mom's closet. I have put everything back exactly how I found it, leaving the key with the safe since it's empty now. I walk out of their bedroom, closing the double doors behind me.

My stomach growls in protest. I'm sure the alcohol mixed with nerves has it upset. I decide on a peanut-butter-and-strawberry-preserve sandwich. It's quick and easy, and right now, I just want another drink to help calm me until Devin is home. Fears of becoming an alcoholic creep into my consciousness, but I don't care. I scarf down my food as if it will be the last meal I ever have with a bottle of water. Instinctively, I grab another tumbler of Jack before heading to my bedroom.

# Chapter Fifteen

The room is cold, and the smell is horrid. I'm hanging onto the edge of the sink that I had recently vomited in after viewing my dad's body. I'm trying to gather myself to view my mother's body on the second table. The creepy doctor keeps telling me that the sooner I do this, the faster I can get out of here. This disgusting stout man has no sympathy or patience, apparently. After taking a couple of deep breaths, I turn to the man, square my shoulders, and look him in his heartless eyes before speaking. "Please wait until I tell you I'm ready this time," I snap with firmness etched in my voice.

"I don't have all day, sweetheart. Four others died on that freeway, you know."

"You're an insensitive piece of shit! Have some fucking compassion for the grieving!" I yell.

A wicked smirk spreads across his face as his yellowed teeth barely show between his chapped lips. My stomach revolts just at the sight of this disgusting man. Just when I think he is about to say something else, he snaps back the sheet on the second table. I jump back. My scream echoes off of the walls, but this time, it isn't a body I'm staring at—it's a viper.

I wake up dripping in sweat. My heart feels as though it wants to break through my chest, and my ears roar as my elevated pulse rushes blood through my head. I lie there on my back, trying to regulate my breathing. Holy shit! It was just another nightmare. Thank God!

My room is lit up by the television and the moon shining through my French doors. Swinging my feet over the edge of my bed, I saunter over to my bathroom but stop short when I see Olivia is outside talking to Devin, standing a little too close for my comfort. Abandoning freshening up in the bathroom, I turn and head out front. Both heads turn when they hear the front door open.

Even though it's dark out, I can see Olivia's perfectly styled fire-engine-red hair and slender body frame covered by a form-fitted black dress, and she's just inches shorter than Devin with her five-inch red stilettos, which match her hair. Why she's dressed to the nines is beyond me.

The only light provided besides the moon is a couple of streetlamps, and I can see Devin's smile light up his face as he watches me approach them. "Hey, baby. I was just getting home when Mrs. Gage stopped me."

"Oh, please, Devin, call me Olivia," she purrs as her hand reaches up to touch his bicep. As I feel the hairs on the back of neck prickle, I can physically see Devin's body tense. I have a sudden urge to smack her hand away from him—or just smack her in general.

As I walk toward Devin, he steps away from Olivia's unwanted touch and wraps his arm around my waist, giving me a kiss at my temple. He looks down at me with concern, as I'm sure he can feel my sweat-damp hair from my recent nightmare, but he has sense enough not to say anything in front of the prying ears of Olivia.

"Olivia, is there something you need?" I ask without any greeting or small talk.

"No, Alexa. I just wanted to meet this handsome young man that has been staying with you." She licks her Botoxed lips as her dark eyes wander shamelessly over Devin's body as if she wants to eat him alive. Another shiver runs down my spine. What in the hell is this woman doing?

"Well, you've met. Good night, Olivia." I turn to walk away, tugging on Devin's hand, leading him back to the house. Again, he's smart enough not to say anything and just follows me.

"I'll be seeing you later, Devin," she calls to our backs in a sultry voice.

I want to turn and tell her no she won't, but I don't want to give her the satisfaction that she's gotten under my skin.

As soon as I have the door shut and locked, I turn on Devin. "What the hell was that?" I ask as calmly as I can.

"I have no fucking clue. I was walking up, and she stopped me. I literally had just told her my name when you walked out. She's not all there, is she?"

"The more interaction I have with the woman, the more I'm beginning to think that she's not."

"Hey, are you alright?" Devin asks as concern furrows his brows.

"Just another nightmare. Nothing to worry about."

"Maybe you should see a therapist. They could probably prescribe something to help you sleep or help with your sudden anxiety attacks. These nightmares are coming more frequently, Lex."

"They come almost every time I close my eyes to sleep," I correct Devin's assessment. "Maybe you're right about therapy, though. I will look into it on Monday. For now, I just want to get through the weekend."

I head into the bathroom to finally freshen up and get ready for bed first. Devin is hungry, so he goes to the kitchen to grab a bite to eat. As I am passing the French doors to head back to my bed, I glance across the way and see a female silhouette in Ethan's window. Why is the crazy bitch spying on me? I will be buying curtains for my doors tomorrow. Olivia is really starting to freak me out.

I crawl into bed and grab my cell phone off the nightstand. I missed a text from Devin telling me he was on his way home, another text from Jess saying that she and Becca were looking forward to seeing me on Saturday, and one last text from an unknown number that simply read: "Always mine."

I send a quick reply back to Jess, and then, after a moment of hesitation, I type a quick reply to the unknown number: "Ethan, is this you?" Just like last time, nothing in return. Oh, well. I delete all my messages, turn the television to Food Network, and settle back in bed. After a few minutes into Chopped, Devin comes in and goes into the bathroom for his nightly ritual. When he emerges from the bathroom, he is only wearing his boxer briefs. My libido immediately reacts to the sight of his lean, athletic body. He crawls into the other side of the bed and scoots closer to me. He pulls me so my head is lying on his chest. His arm wraps around my shoulders, and my leg rests over his as we snuggle into each other. I feel his lips brush a soft kiss to the top of my head.

"Good night, baby. I love you," he whispers.

"Dev?"

"Yeah?"

"Stay away from Olivia, please. Something isn't right, and I don't want you near her."

"You don't have to ask me twice," he says, placing another kiss on my head, his arm tightening around me.

After a few moments pass, I lean my head up and kiss the underside of his jaw. "I love you, Devin."

"Mmm" is all I get out of him. His breathing is even and light, and I can tell he's already asleep. I wish it were that simple for me to fall asleep, but since it's not, I continue to watch Chopped.

# Chapter Sixteen

It's Friday, and the day seems to be flying by so quickly with all the preparations for my parents' remembrance celebration taking place the following day. George and Marie both took the day off to help with, well, everything.

Marie and Devin are dealing with the party supply rental company. Devin shows the tent crew where to set up the raised platform and structure on the lawn, as other people are bustling around me with tables, chairs, folded red linens, and who knows what else. Marie instructs the staff as to where the buffet table and bar should be set up once the platform is built. My mind is spinning with all the chaos. I have to keep reminding myself to breathe.

I was grateful that I went to the bank first thing in the morning to get the money from the safe deposit box after speaking with a gentleman my dad had already lined up to do the finishing touches on the AC Cobra we were building. The man gave me his condolences and said that he would be happy to complete the rest of the car for me even though it's more work than anticipated. He assured me he would be by around noon to pick up my project. I'm nervous because I know there is something extremely top secret hidden in the car, but I can't let anyone know about it and I can't move it now. There are too many people around, and I don't want to chance anyone seeing me in the garage. It's killing me that I can't even tell Devin about it.

It's just after noon when George helps Mr. Belles with loading the Cobra onto the flatbed truck. Of course the car would catch the attention of most of the workers who are setting up for the event, and suddenly, my anxiety rears its ugly head and I almost pass out from hyperventilating, but I quickly recover and pray no one was paying attention to me. I wish the car was a little more inconspicuous, but that's not reality. An hour later, Mr. Belles is on his way with everything loaded securely from the back garage. He told me I am welcome at the shop anytime to check on the car or even to assist if I want to. Come to find out Mr. Belles is another person my dad has known for quite some time but I have never met. I'm positive I will check on the car, but not for reasons Mr. Belles will assume I am there for.

By four, the backyard had been completely transformed. The grass area has a large platform where a dozen tables are arranged with six chairs around each table under a large white tent with twinkling chandeliers hanging strategically throughout. We opted for the tent since the weather forecast predicted rain over the weekend and we couldn't take any chances. I didn't want all these people in my house. The buffet tables and bar are set up on the left side of the platform, and a DJ station is across the entrance at the back of the tent. Flowers will arrive in the morning to add to the ambiance. If the rain holds off, people will be able to mingle throughout the whole backyard, but by the looks of the darkening clouds above, I won't be so lucky.

Devin comes up behind me and wraps his arms around my waist as I stand taking in everything that has been transformed in my backyard. "You OK, Lex?" he whispers in my ear before placing a soft kiss right where my neck meets my shoulder, sending goose bumps down my arms.

I rest my arms over his and turn my head to look up at him. "I just want tomorrow to be over. I want my privacy. This is a bit overwhelming. I didn't realize it was going to be this much work. I'm just glad your parents are handling the majority of the preparation."

I turn in his arms and wrap myself into the warmth of his body, resting my head on his chest. His grip tightens around my shoulders, comforting me. He feels so good, and the clean, woodsy scent that is uniquely Devin is intoxicating. He brings his hands up to my face and leans down to kiss me. It's sweet, gentle, and emotionally charged. His left hand grips my hair at the nape of my neck as his right hand slides down just at the top of my backside.

"Eh-hem," George interrupts our moment, again. At least this is not as embarrassing as before. "We're heading home. We will be back by nine in the morning to help with the florist and caterer. And, Lexi, we know tomorrow is going to be extremely hard on you and your emotions. Do not feel pressured to stay out here to socialize. Marie and I are more than happy to make sure everyone has a good time if you find that you need a break."

"Thank you both so much. You mean the world to me, and I'm thankful to have you in my life." I step out of Devin's embrace and walk over to hug George. He pulls me into a big bear hug, and I swear I hear his breath hitch. I know this is hard on everyone, but watching a grown man cry would be enough to shatter what little strength I have holding me together. He releases me, and I turn to hug Marie.

"We love you, honey," she whispers in my ear as a tear trickles down my cheek.

"Come on, my love. Let's leave these two to rest up for tomorrow. Lord knows we are all going to need it." And with that being said, they are gone.

We head into the house and plop down in the family room, exhausted. After channel surfing, we decide to watch Freddy vs. Jason since it just happens to be on TV. I'm snuggled up to Devin on the couch with my head resting on his shoulder. My hand is playing with the hem of his shirt. I slide it under the material and begin lightly tickling his rock-hard abs. I feel him flex as a hiss escapes his lips. I quickly find myself on my back, pressed into the couch as Devin's body perfectly covers mine and his mouth claims mine. His tongue flicks into my mouth, brushing against my tongue. On cue, my core tightens as I feel my arousal wetting my panties.

Devin unbuttons and unzips my jeans quickly, sliding them down my legs. I have just enough time to release only one of my legs from my jeans before he lifts my shirt and begins trailing kisses down my flat stomach and across my pubic bone and rips away the scrap of material that was my thong. His tongue gently licks up my moistened seam, causing my hips to buck upward, a moan escaping at the same time. I hear a feral growl come from between my legs as he tastes me for the first time. He repeats the motions a few more times as I wiggle beneath him, before I feel one of his hands trying to hold me steady as his soft, warm tongue plunges deep between my folds. My hands fly into his hair, gripping it tight as his mouth devours my sex. He slides two fingers inside me as his tongue swirls around my clit.

"Holy fuck," I gasp. "Dev, I'm. Going. To. Come." My breathy voice shakes as I feel the now familiar tightening of my core and my pussy grips at the fingers he's skillfully fucking me with. He turns his hand so that the pads of his fingers can hit that sensitive spot at the front of my sex. Just as he does this maneuver, his teeth lightly graze my throbbing clit, and then immediately, his tongue is back to swirling my nub, sending me over the threshold of pure sexual bliss. My grip on Devin's hair keeps him firmly placed at my sex as I ride out my orgasm. His head is being squeezed like a vice by my thighs.

I finally release my sex induced death grip on Devin, and he quickly moves his body up mine, kissing me gently. I can taste myself on his lips, and for some reason, that is such a turn-on for me.

"Was that as good for you as it was for me?" Devin asks as his stormy blue eyes stare down at me.

"That was—oh, my God," I reply with a goofy grin on my face since I can't seem to find the word or words to tell him exactly how amazing that felt.

His boyish smile brightens his eyes as I pull his lips back to mine.

"I've been dying to taste you, and, woman, you taste divine."

"Take me to bed and make love to me," I whisper in his ear.

Just like that, Devin stands and leans down to pick me up, cradling me with my jeans still dangling from one leg as he carries me two flights of stairs to my room, our room. We spend the next two hours making love.

Greeting the guests and having to endure the continuous words of condolences mixed with sympathy and looks of pity has me wanting these people gone. When my father's boss and a couple of his co-workers approached I was actually afraid they would ask me about the files but they didn't. They just offered the same condolences as everyone else.

I am finally seated at a table alone with only the twins. People continue to mingle all around me, but my attention remains solely at our table. Just as the weatherman predicted, it's raining. Luckily, it's a light rain, but it is still enough to keep all the guests in the tented area.

Sitting between Jessa and Becca, I've told them pretty much everything that has happened since the earthquake. Both girls called me a slut since I admitted to having sex with Ethan and then Devin a couple of days later, but they said it jokingly. They understand now that they know the whole story—well, everything aside from the memory card and a man named Viper who may or may not show up in my life.

"I can't believe the fucker took your virginity and then bailed to

Seattle with no phone call, text, or anything." Becca's voice is a little louder than I want it to be. Thankfully, the DJ had the big band music just loud enough that the guests nearest our table didn't hear her.

"It is what it is. If he hadn't left, I probably wouldn't be with Devin," I reply honestly as I glance around the room, looking briefly for my amazing boyfriend before our eyes lock. His smile meant just for me brightens his handsome features and gives me a sense of calm.

"Oh, barf," Jess mutters as she rolls her eyes. "Look at you two, all lovey-dovey. Is this what we get to look forward to when you guys are at school?" she asks, making me smile my first sincere smile of the day.

"You better believe it." I nudge her shoulder with mine. "I love you two skanks, you know that, right?" I say to both as tears begin to well in my eyes. My chest tightens, and I feel an ache grip my heart. I've missed them terribly but I've been caught up in my grief, the whirlwind that was Ethan Gage, and reuniting with Devin. I'm just glad they are so understanding and that they now know everything. Now I feel like I can breathe and my best friends and I can start getting back to life as usual.

"Oh, Lex, of course we do. We love you too," Becca says, gripping my hand in an effort to comfort me. Within seconds, I feel Devin's strong hands rest on my shoulders. His presence soothes my overwhelming emotions, and right now, all I want is to be alone with him, locked away in our little bubble.

Devin bends down, his warm breath tickling my neck as he whispers, "You OK, baby? If you want to go inside, I will go with you. My parents have this under control."

I nod at Devin. "Could you please let them know?" I whisper back.

"Of course. I will be right back," Devin says as he places a kiss on my temple before heading to find his parents.

"Jess, Becca, I think I'm going to go inside. Please stay and enjoy the party with your parents and give them my apologies for not saying good-bye in person. I just need some peace and quiet for a little bit." I stare at both apologetically.

"Oh, is that what you're calling it," Jess says, making me snort laughter through my tears.

"You always know the right or wrong thing to say to make me laugh." We all stand, and I give them hugs before slipping out of the tent, hopefully unseen.

As I step inside the sliding glass door, I run right into the svelte frame of Olivia. My body automatically tenses at her mere presence. "What are you doing here, Olivia?" I ask in a curt tone.

"I just wanted to come pay my respects, Alexa," she replies nonchalantly.

"You've done that already. Please leave my house," I seethe.

"As you wish, dear." Her voice chills. "Please tell that gorgeous boy of yours I said hello," she says over her shoulder as she sashays up the stairs toward the front door. My entire body is coiled with anger. What game is this horrid woman playing?

I hear her mumbled voice before the door closes, and I walk up the stairs to head to my bedroom when I stop abruptly at the top to find a very big military-looking man standing by the front door. I swallow back the lump in my throat as I take in the very large, muscular man dressed in all black standing in front of me. My eyes immediately go to his left hand, but he's wearing gloves so I can't tell if he is who I think he is.

Removing his gloves, as if to answer my unspoken question, he asks, "Alexa, I presume?" He has an English accent.

I still can't see the top of his left hand, and I know he can sense I'm struggling to see it, so he extends it in effort to shake my hand. Just as he does, his jacket and shirt sleeve rise up his wrist just enough to show the snake tattoo perfectly. For being on the hand and partially up the wrist, the detail is quite impressive. The tattoo colors are unexpectedly vibrant. The viper's body is intricately scaly with yellow, green, and red, and it is in a coiled position as if ready to strike out.

I finally bring my attention up to the chiseled face of the man in front of me as I extend my tiny hand to shake his. "Yes. I'm Alexa, or Lexi," I answer with a shaky voice.

"Ms. Morgan, I'm Sebastian Bentley, a friend of your father's," he introduces himself.

I tilt my head in confusion at first, but then my brain kicks in. Well, duh, his real name isn't Viper.

"It's a pleasure to meet you. My dad mentioned I might."

"Is there someplace we can talk in private?" he asks.

"Today is really not a good day for privacy. As you can see, it's my parents' remembrance party, and people are everywhere," I offer apologetically.

"Ah, that it is. Please accept my apologies and condolences. I didn't mean to intrude."

"I can assure you that you are not intruding; you have just caught me off guard. You are more than welcome to join the party out back. I was just coming inside for a much-needed break."

"I don't think that would be wise, but thank you for the offer. Actually, I will be flying out later tonight for a few months, and I just wanted to make your acquaintance before I did so and also to be sure all is good." His hazel eyes stare at me, hoping I catch the cryptic code.

Devin comes running up the stairs just as I am going to answer. He stops short, taking in the scene in front of him. "Lex, is everything OK?" he asks, eyeing the man in a fitted black suit with a black dress shirt under the jacket. I didn't even see that he put his gloves back on. My guess is to conceal the tattoo.

"Everything is fine. This is Sebastian Bentley. He was a friend of my father's. He just wanted to stop by before he left for the airport." Oh God, did I just give too much information?

Devin reaches out to shake Viper's hand and exchange pleasantries.

"Alexa, I will be in touch when I return. I'm glad everything is taken care of. Here is my business card. You can call me if you ever need anything. Your father was a good man, and I promised I would make myself available if you ever needed guidance."

This guy is good. I'm just shocked I can actually read through all the cryptic messages. It must be all those spy movies my dad and I watched together. Then it hit me. Is this guy a spy? Did my dad have a secret life I never knew about? Fifteen other questions started rattling around in my brain but something tells me I will never get the answers I seek.

"Thank you, Mr. Bentley. I will." I smile at the man as he turns to leave out the front door.

"Well, he seems, uh, nice," Devin says when we're alone.

"Not at all what I expected," I say as I continue up to my room. Oh, shit! How would I expect anything of a man I just met? I hope Dev doesn't catch my second slipup.

Either Devin didn't catch it or he's just ignoring my comment, which eases my nerves a bit. I crawl onto my bed and lie down with my back toward Devin's side of the bed. After closing the double doors to the room, he lies down behind me, pulling my backside into his front, and wraps his strong arms securely around me. I must have been exhausted because I don't remember a thing after lying down.

# Chapter Seventeen

## Eight Months Later

The first couple of months after my parents' deaths were extremely difficult. Ongoing anytime-my-eyes-are-closed-mares, anxiety, Olivia's craziness coming to the forefront more often, and weekly text messages from a different unknown number each time haven't helped my grieving process, but being in therapy and having Devin by my side have helped tremendously. I cannot believe how caring, loving, and attentive Devin is. I'm a very lucky girl to have my best friend as my boyfriend. I also can't believe how far we've come in such a short period of time. I couldn't imagine my life without him, which has only fueled some of my anxiety attacks. My parents' sudden deaths are a constant reminder that something could happen to Devin just as easily, and then I would really be left all alone. I shake my head slightly, as if it would help clear away my unwanted thoughts. Today is supposed to be a happy day, and I keep repeating that to myself.

Devin and I are standing side by side, each at our own bathroom sink, as we both finish getting ready for our graduation. I decided to wear a baby-blue maxi skirt with a white sleeveless button-down top. I chose the outfit because, as I was cleaning out my mom's closet the other day, I found a pair of baby-blue with white stripes Jimmy Choo lace-up platform sandals. Her designer shoes always made me happy and feel pretty when I would borrow them, grateful we wore the same size. I couldn't bear parting with a single pair of her shoes or any of her bags. Devin teased me, reminding me of when I used to be a tomboy. That feels like ages ago. As for my mom's clothes, I donated everything to the women's shelter.

My dad's things were a little harder to go through. I kept all of his San Francisco 49ers and Giants jerseys and T-shirts, as well as his favorite classic rock band Journey T-shirt. I sleep in that one most often, if I'm not sleeping in the nude. Everything else went to the Salvation Army. I did, however, keep every piece of jewelry they owned. Anything that wasn't costume jewelry went into my safe deposit box at the bank. I was thankful to get both of their wedding rings back after the accident, and I keep my dad's around my neck on a silver chain. It somehow comforts me.

I glance over at Devin through the reflection in the mirror. He's wearing a pair of faded boot-cut jeans that are just tight enough to accentuate his firm ass. The simple tight black T-shirt shows off almost every muscle in his upper body through the thin material. His blonder-than-normal hair is spiked messily with gel, and his blue eyes shine like they always do after he comes deep inside me. Licking my lips, I suddenly have the need to close my thighs tight as my panties moisten from that last thought.

Devin's eyes lock with mine in the mirror as he smirks. "Baby, if you keep staring at me like you want to fuck me again, we will be late for our graduation. I can barely restrain myself as it is from bending you over the sink and taking you from behind." His voice is huskily laced with a heady aspiration to be intimate with me.

That is my breaking point. I don't care if we are going to be late. I tug at his jeans buttons, undoing them quickly. I slide his jeans along with his boxer briefs down just far enough to release his already stiff erection. I drag my bottom lip through my teeth as I wrap my hand around Devin's substantial girth, stroking him a few times before he spins me so my palms rest flat on my makeup vanity. Devin quickly lifts my skirt up around my waist and rips away my thong, leaving me open and bare for him.

"Fuck, Lexi, you are already glistening with your arousal," he murmurs as he sinks two fingers inside me, working them in and out of me to prep me for his steel shaft. My hips thrust back to meet his hand as my sex clenches around him.

A moan escapes my lips as I beg, "I want you inside me now."

He removes his fingers, and my eyes are fixed on watching us through the reflection of the mirror when I feel the crest of his cock slip through my swollen folds. He steadies himself before he pushes forward, sinking all the way in. Watching his expression turn animalistic is the most erotic thing I've ever seen. Devin throws his head back with a guttural growl, and his fingers dig deeper into the flesh of my hips as he sets the punishing pace inside my pussy.

"Oh God, Dev. Don't stop. Harder," I plead as I reach down to rub my clit in an effort to help reach my orgasm faster.

His eyes snap to mine. "That is so fucking hot, watching you play with yourself. Lex, I'm not going to last much longer, baby."

I pick up the pace, rubbing my clit faster in a circular motion as my ass cheeks slap against Devin's thighs. His eyes stay bared to mine as they grow darker with his imminent release. He reaches one hand up, cupping my breast through my top, pinching my budded nipple. Everything inside me tightens all at once, and my orgasm thunders through me. My pussy grips Devin's length like a vice, and just as quickly as my orgasm struck me, his rocks through him. He grunts out the words "fuck me," followed by a distorted version of my name between uneven breaths as his release shoots deep into my velvety walls as the head of his penis hits my cervix. His softening member faintly twitches inside me a couple more times as Devin completely drains himself.

We are both trying to catch our breaths and steady our racing hearts when my phone chimes with a text from Becca, telling us to hurry up and get to the field in not-so-sweet words. With postorgasmic shaky hands, I send a quick response back, letting her know that we are leaving the house in a few minutes.

I grab my hand towel to clean the come that is dripping down my inner thighs. Once I'm dry enough, I straighten my skirt, making sure I don't have too many wrinkles as Devin pulls his boxer briefs and jeans back up to his hips, tucking his semihard shaft away.

"You're not going to wash up?" I ask with an arched brow.

"Nah, this way, I can smell you all through the ceremony." He smirks, leaning over and placing a chaste kiss on my flushed cheek.

"What?" I ask, shocked.

He just stands with his arms folded across his chest and his shiny blues dancing with mischief.

"I'll never get enough of you. You realize that, right?" I tell him.

"I hope you don't because I know I will always want you, Alexa. I love you," he replies, unfolding from his previous stance and placing a sweet kiss to my lips. "Now go put on another pair of panties and let's go. We're running late," he chides playfully as he turns me toward the bathroom door and swats me on the ass, making me yelp.

"Well, damn, Dev. I was just thinking I might go commando." I wink at him as I exit the bathroom.

He's following me out the door when he replies, "Do you want me sitting through graduation with a constant hard-on, Lex? That's just mean." He laughs.

"Well, you are apparently OK with sitting through the ceremony with the scent of our sexual encounter, so why not?" I joke. "But, no, I wouldn't want that, baby," I say over my shoulder as I go into my closet to put on another pair of panties.

Devin grabs our caps and gowns from the bed, and we head down to the garage. Just after Devin officially moved in, I sold my dad's car because I didn't need it. Mom's car was totaled in the accident so the insurance money just went into the bank with all my other money. For a brief moment, I thought about keeping my dad's Audi A7, but my A3 was better suited for me. I walk past my car and Devin's Audi A5 and Chevelle before I finally reach the driver's side of the blue-with-white-stripes '65 AC Shelby Cobra kit car that my dad and I started to build together. Mr. Belles had finished the car for me, since I couldn't pull myself to complete the car without my dad. Mr. Belles did a beautiful job, though. Every week that he had the car, I would go over and visit with him for an hour or so. Each time, I would secretly check to make sure the micro-SD card was still where I had hid it. Now that the car is home with me, I check for it every day.

Just as I go to slide in the driver's seat, I hear Devin say, "Hey, uh-uh. I'm driving today."

I throw my head back with a genuine laugh as I continue to sit my butt in the driver's seat. "Oh, baby, you can drive me anytime you want, but I'm driving her," I tease back, patting the dashboard.

"You're lucky I love you," he says with narrowed eyes as he gets into the car on the passenger side.

A victorious smile spreads across my lips, and I lean over, taking Devin's face in one hand. I bring his lips to mine for a quick kiss.

"I love you too," I say against his lips before pulling away, buckling up, and starting the car. She rumbles to life. Her vibrations give me goose bumps every time I drive her. I hope that feeling never goes away. My dad was right though—I always have a silly grin when I'm behind the wheel of this magnificent machine, and I really do feel like he is with me.

I ease her out of the garage and back down the driveway. I little pang of sadness hits when I see the "Sold" sign on my front lawn. A couple of months ago, Devin and I decided the house was too big for just the two of us, and with Olivia giving us both the creeps, I put my house on the market. Thank goodness the housing market was on the rise. There was a bidding war, and I ended up getting sixty thousand over asking. I didn't need the money, but it was nice to be banking a hefty sum. Once all was said and done, my parents really did make sure I would want for nothing. I probably wouldn't need to work a day in my life if I didn't want to, but I had my heart set on counseling abused and troubled kids.

Once the house sold, Devin and I agreed that we would be better off moving closer to Stanford. We found a cute three-bedroom Eichler-style home close to campus and downtown Palo Alto. Even though the house was in desperate need of renovations, which should be complete by the beginning of July, the deciding factor to choose that particular house was the large separate garage behind the main house. It will be the new home for the Chevelle and Cobra, while our everyday drivers will share the attached garage. The backyard had a hot tub in a Japanese garden setting that made it Zen-like and serene. Whoever owned the house prior didn't care about the inside, but both the front yard and backyard were lavishly landscaped. We will definitely be hiring a gardener since neither of us have a clue about gardening. I'm pretty sure I wouldn't even be able to keep a fake plant alive.

Devin senses my sudden unease and wraps his hand over the one I have resting on the shifter. I smile over at him before continuing to back the car farther while turning her.

"I should have worn my Chucks to drive. It's hard to push the clutch in with these platform sandals."

"I'm more than happy to drive, Lex," he says with his megawatt smile that shows his barely there dimple I adore.

"Nice try with that sexy smile of yours, but no go," I say as we turn and rumble down the street.

It feels as though we make it to the school football stadium in record time in this car. Not only was I slightly speeding, which isn't hard to do in this car, but I even had a motors officer nod appreciation as I roared by him at an intersection.

"We would have been pulled over if you were driving," I say to Devin as we pull into the parking lot. People's heads turn to see the source of the rumbling that is echoing through the lot.

"Yeah, because I wouldn't have been driving like a grandma," he teases me.

I reach over and smack his arm when I spot the twins with their parents waving at us and pointing to an open spot, which I ease the car into.

"Amazing car, Alexa," Mr. Ritchfield says in admiration.

"Thanks, Mr. Ritchfield. It was my dad's dream car."

The twins give both me and Devin hugs, and just as they do, we hear Principal Cassidy's voice over the PA system, asking parents, friends, and family of the graduates to take their seats as the senior class lines up. We start to head toward the field when we hear George's voice. "Hey, Son," he says from behind us as he and Marie approach.

"Hi, Mom, Dad," Devin says, giving both parents a hug.

"Alexa, you look beautiful as ever," Marie compliments as she hugs me.

"Thanks, although I'm a little windblown and smell like the Cobra since I drove her today." I nod toward the car.

"Worth the knotted hair, though, isn't it?" George beams with appreciation as he looks over at the curvy vehicle.

"Most definitely! Your son pouted the entire way because I wouldn't let him drive," I say jokingly, making everyone laugh at Devin's expense. He suddenly grabs me around the waist, pulling me into his firm body as his mouth captures mine in a passionate kiss that makes my toes curl.

"Get a room!" Becca shouts as we reluctantly break apart.

"They are always like this," Jessa complains to Devin's parents.

"Oh, we know. We have a few stories to tell after graduation," George says as he grabs his son playfully in a headlock. Devin breaks free, and the two men pretend to start boxing, boyish grins plastered on both of their faces. It warms me to watch them play.

Devin, the twins, and I head over to where the senior class is lining up as both sets of parents make their way to the stands. Devin stays with me in the line since there are only four people whose names are between ours.

Lately, I feel as though someone is watching me, and I glance around our current surroundings, but I don't see anything out of the ordinary. Then again, there are so many people and a lot going on that this isn't necessarily ordinary. I've felt this way for a couple of days now and even mentioned it to my therapist. He suggested that it could be because of graduation and wishing my parents were here to see me graduate. Although his explanation would be a valid one, in my mind, I think it could also be because Mr. Bentley, or Viper, contacted me five days ago, informing me that he would be back in California in the middle of July and would like to meet with me then. I agreed and gave him my new address. I know I'm just being paranoid, but the nagging feeling of being watched won't go away. I wrap my arms around Devin's waist, hoping his embrace will help ease the anxiety that is building in me. I stopped taking all of my prescription medications a month ago because I didn't like how I felt when I would take them, but today, I could have used them. Who was I kidding, thinking I didn't need them anymore?

"Don't worry, baby. You won't trip and fall," Devin whispers in my ear, thinking my nervousness has to do with walking the stage to get my diploma.

"Thanks for the vote of confidence," I snap back as his low chuckle vibrates through his chest. Well, I wasn't worried about tripping before, but I am now.

An hour and a half later, we are all officially graduated and will be college bound in the fall. The twins will both be attending Santa Clara University while Devin and I are at Stanford. Finding out Becca and Jessa are staying local made me happy, since they will still be close enough to hang out often. I don't know what would have happened to me if these three people standing here weren't in my life when my parents died. I owe them all so much, and words will never be enough to explain my endless gratitude.

The Ritchfields and Millers have both found our little group in the middle of all the postgraduate chaos. Seniors are running around hugging each other and saying their good-byes. We've been bombarded a few dozen times. Devin's parents take a picture of just Devin and me first and then one with us and the twins. Jessa asks Devin to take a picture of her and Becca with their parents, and that's when I decide to excuse myself to go to the restroom. My anxiety mixed with me wishing my parents were here sharing this day like everyone else's is making me feel nauseous. I don't want to be a downer on graduation day. We have dinner planned with Devin's and the twins' families, and then we're headed to a couple of parties. I really just need a moment to gather myself.

Devin grabs my hand before I am out of reach, and I turn to look up into his blue eyes. "Want me to go with you?" he asks, concerned.

"No. I'm fine. I just need to use the restroom," I lie.

He knows I'm lying, but he would never call me on it in front of anyone. If anyone would know how hard today is for me, it would be him.

He kisses my forehead and releases my hand. I walk over to the restrooms, or shall I say, Porta-Potties, and the lines for each one are long. I know where another set of blue rooms is hidden, since I found them at one of the many football games I had gone to. Ever since Devin transferred schools, my Saturday nights were spent in the stands with Becca and Jessa cheering on Devin and of course the rest of our team.

Strolling around the back of the locked-up concessions building, I make my way down a little pathway when I feel a strong arm wrap around my waist, pulling me to his body. The hand that is splayed on my stomach is placed in a possessive manner. I instinctively think Devin followed me, but the rigid body against my back feels different, yet familiar.

His lips brush against my ear, and his warm breath smells of whiskey as he whispers, "Mine."

My breath escapes my lungs as I feel every inch of my body, every fiber of my being, react to his touch, his voice, of how he possesses me. Heat pools deep in my belly, and all I can think is, How can my body betray me like this? More so, how can it betray Devin, the man I love, like this?

I turn around slowly, coming face-to-face with liquid gray eyes blazing with a hunger that I recognize from months ago. The gorgeous man who stands before me can still take my breath away, literally. Once my brain starts to function again, and I regain some composure, the only word that escapes my lips is, "Ethan."

# Epilogue

## Ethan

Ever since the day I left California and spinelessly left Lexi, I have regretted it. I know Olivia is monitoring my e-mails, cell phone, and everything else I do, so I had to be smart about how I would contact Alexa. I never know who is on Olivia's payroll or if she hired a full-time private investigator to babysit me because she is that bat-shit crazy and possessive.

Fuck! I just want to hear Lexi's sweet voice or even just a text to help with this fucked situation that is my life. I want to hold her close and smell the strawberry-vanilla scent that is uniquely her. I want to feel the sexy curves of her body pressed against my body. God, she is beautiful and perfect. I can still hear her moan and imagine the feel of her pussy tightening around my fingers when I gave her her very first orgasm. Just the thought of her velvety warmth is making my dick hard. Those vivid thoughts have plagued my memory the last couple of days, and I can either take another cold shower or jerk off to the memory of my Lexi. I think I will go with the latter. At least some release is better than having even more pent-up frustration from blue balls.

Now that my mind is a little clearer from my one-on-one with myself, I can head out to the little market by the hotel. I have gone in a couple of times for some Jack Daniel's, since the market is least likely to be monitored. The last time I went in, I overheard a man ask for a throwaway phone. The shady character behind the counter said it was twenty bucks. The guy handed him a twenty and walked out. This is my chance to at least text Lexi to let her know I'm thinking about her, so I walk in and glance around. After seeing we are the only two people in the store, I ask the guy behind the counter for a throwaway phone. He eyes me suspiciously, and I immediately think he is on Olivia's payroll, but he nods and tells me it's twenty bucks. I hand him a twenty, and he quickly informs me that these phones are usually good for one or two brief calls and a couple of text messages. I nod my understanding. I only need it to work once. Before leaving the market, I turn back and ask the guy for a fifth of Jack, and he rings me up legitimately for the alcohol. I pay him and hurry back to my room. Once I'm back, I lock myself in the bathroom, turn on the shower, and type out my only text to Lexi: MINE. That one word speaks volumes, and she will know exactly what it means. Lexi is mine and will always be mine.

I wait about fifteen minutes, and disappointment settles as I get nothing in return. Fuck! I turn off the water and wait another five minutes before stepping out of the bathroom. I carefully open the door to my hotel room and glance out, relieved to see only the maid's cart a few doors down, so I walk down and toss the garbage-bag-wrapped phone into the wastebasket of the maid's cart and head back to my room.

It's been about forty minutes since I threw away the phone, and I hear a faint chime sound right outside my door. I glance through the peephole and see the cart across the hall. I immediately wonder if it was my throwaway phone, so I swing open the door, but before I can dig into the wastebasket, I spot a man sitting at the end of the hall with a newspaper, eyeing me. I know for sure he's my assigned babysitter, as I've seen him a few times already. I cross the hall, peeking my head into the open room, and ask the maid if it's OK if I grab a couple of extra towels. She smiles at me and nods, gesturing to help myself. Once I have grabbed the towels, I turn and retreat back into my room. I will never know for sure if it was Lexi responding to my text. My only hope is that it was and that she still wants me and misses me as much as I need and miss her.

Fuck my life.

# Author Biography

T.R. Cupak was born and raised in the suburbs of a Bay Area city in California. She was the closet nerd who hid her love of reading and writing short stories and poetry when she was younger. Back then it wasn't considered cool to be into those types of activities for pleasure, whereas today you have TV shows, movies and books that glamourize that being a nerd is actually cool.

T. lives in a quiet, little, country town south of where she grew up. She is happily married to an amazing man who supports her in everything she does and spoils her rotten. They have a crazy little Shih Tzu named Harley. He's their fur-baby and even though he's a pain in the arse most days, they love the little guy. She has an obsession with cars, especially fast ones. She enjoys her music louder than anyone should. Admittedly it's to drown out hearing her own singing voice, or lack thereof. When she's not at work or busy writing you can find her curled up reading a book on her Kindle with a glass of wine or Dirty Shirley.

T. lost touch with her creative side and stepped off the path of all things written in her early twenties. Six years ago, her passion for reading was rekindled. She began to utilize reading as a way to escape everyday chaos. Late 2013 she began journal writing. After a couple of months of journaling T. realized that this form of writing wasn't keeping her interest nor was it helping her to relax. After that realization settled in she changed the direction of her writing. Her creative aspirations were flowing once again and she happily embraced it. As her fingers started to dance across her keyboard she began to see her fictional characters begin to breathe life. Writing was only supposed to be a way for the new author to relax, but a story was born and T.R. Cupak is excited to be releasing her self-published debut novel, *Alexa Crushed*.